CW00569676

Sundown at Singing River

Recognizing that the era of his profession has ended, gunfighter Jorje Katz rides into the town of Singing River to begin a new life. On arrival he discovers that the partner he had financed is long dead, and with no money to his name, his only option is to become a hired gun in a war that is raging between two political factions in the town.

Dragged back into his old ways, but with a woman to remind him just how good life can be, he despairs until he is appointed Sheriff of Singing River. At last it seems that his dreams can finally be realized. . . .

Sundown at Singing River

Ty Kirwan

ROBERT HALE · LONDON

First published in Great Britain 2012

ISBN 978-0-7090-9480-7

Robert Hale Limited
Clerkenwell House
Clerkenwell Green
London EC1R 0HT

www.halebooks.com

Typeset by
Derek Doyle & Associates, Shaw Heath
Printed and bound in Great Britain by
CPI Antony Rowe, Chippenham and Eastbourne

ONE

On a wet, dismal and uncomfortable night a man walked into the Goldliner Saloon in the town of Singing River. The smell of stale beer dregs and unwashed human beings had him pause briefly inside the door. Having been established for a number of years the town rarely encountered strangers, so the cowboys, miners, gamblers with the squirrel tail of their profession attached to their hats, and saloon girls of varied shapes and sizes, turned to study the newcomer with interest.

In his thirties, of average height, strongly built, ruggedly handsome and with a Colt.45 in a tied-down holster at his right hip, the stranger belonged to a fast fading era. For some of those present he seemed to have stepped out of a hazardous, bloody, violent way of life unlikely to ever be witnessed again except for on a battlefield. Though many of the townsfolk had all but forgotten what a gunfighter looked like, they realized that they were seeing one now. This increased both their nervousness and interest in him but he ignored the attention he was receiving and walked to the bar. A young black-haired girl with a lovely face not yet prematurely aged by her profession, swinging-hipped her way across the room with a sense of timing that had her reach the bar at the same time as the newcomer did.

'I am Carmencita,' she coquettishly introduced herself. 'Are you going to buy me a drink, *amigo*?'

For a time he appeared not to have heard the girl. Then he turned his head to silently study her for a long moment. She wore a short yellow jacket that was undone, black stockings, fancy garters, white shoes, and nothing else other than a long-bladed knife secured by her left garter.

'If I could afford to buy a drink, miss, I would buy it for myself,' he told her in a low-pitched voice.

Her mercenary overture thwarted, the girl twisted her full, red lips into a contemptuous sneer as she flounced off. Ignoring her reaction, he beckoned to a bartender. 'I am looking for a prospector, an old guy who goes by the name of Jasper Coker. Is he in here tonight?'

'I wouldn't know him if he was, mister,' the bartender replied, looking around to beckon an elderly man sitting at a table with two other miners. The old guy rose stiff-bodied from his chair and made his way to the bar on crooked legs.

'What's to do, Mick?' he asked the barkeep after accurately and noisily hitting a spittoon with a chaw of tobacco.

'This man's looking for a prospector name Jasper Coker. D'you know anything of him, Gilbert?'

Squinting at the stranger, the oldster asked, 'What would Jasper be to you, pard?'

'He's my partner. He came out ahead of me to stake a claim.'

'Well I sure as damnit have some real bad news for you, pard. Jasper caught himself one hell of a bad cold at the diggings, and he breathed his last some three months past. Found himself a hole in ground at last, but there sure weren't no darn gold in thar.'

The poker-faced stranger inquired. 'He never did stake a claim?'

'Right sorry to disappoint you, pard, but that's right. You don't look like no prospector to me, but anyway you're a mite late in getting here. Every worthwhile claim has been staked, and just about every one of the hopefuls who lost out has long gone off to seek their fortunes over the far side of the hills.'

'Thank you kindly,' the stranger said, surprising both the oldster and the barkeep by flashing a fine smile.

He was turning away when a well-dressed, suave, polished man with a thin moustache partially blocked his path. Plainly a man of means and importance, he spoke in an educated manner that went with his smart appearance.

'Forgive me for intruding on your privacy, sir, but I couldn't help overhearing your exchange with old Gilbert. You seem to me to be a man down on his luck.'

'I'll survive,' the stranger said, side-stepping in preparation for walking by.

'Excuse me, sir,' the sophisticated man was persistent. 'Permit me to introduce myself. I am Bartholomew Cusick, a man of importance here in Singing River, even if I say so myself. Correct me if I am mistaken, you are Jorje Katz.'

'You are mistaken.'

The stranger walked away with his back towards Cusick, who let him put some distance between them before uttering a sharp one-word challenge. 'Katz!'

In an incredibly fast move, the stranger spun on his heel, drawing his gun as he turned in a crouch, his .45 aimed at Cusick. Some of the saloon's patrons rose quickly to their feet in fear. After a chorus of startled exclamations, a silence, eerie in its depth and suddenness, fell on the assembly.

'Well I'll be all-fired!' a voice made loud by breaking the silence, exclaimed in wonder. 'That was greased lightning.'

Old Gilbert the gold miner advised the speaker. 'Anyone

try to tell you he's seen faster then he's a gosh-darned liar.'

Cusick remained cool in what, to the onlookers, was a perilous situation. Smiling, he had raised both hands in spoof surrender, saying. 'That proves that I know *of* you even if I don't know you. I have a proposition for you, but I'm never at my best when discussing business while looking down the barrel of a firearm. Believe me; it would be to our mutual advantage if you would take a drink with me.'

There was a concerted sigh of relief from the nearest spectators as the gunfighter used a thumb to ease the hammer of his gun forward. He slowly reholstered the weapon, a move that had those around him relax and the general crowd sound start up. The clinking of glasses set up a fitful accompaniment to the vocalization of a girl who had stood on a table to sing.

The stranger walked to the bar with Cusick through air that was bluish with smoke of cigarettes, which both the men and saloon girls indulged in.

'Whiskey?' Cusick asked.

The stranger answered with a nod, and Cusick ordered drinks for them both, saying. 'I should first explain that I was a much-travelled man before settling here in the good town of Singing River. To the best of my knowledge it was in Santa Fe that you came to my notice, in a most impressive manner. I will not go into detail about that now, except to say that the moment you walked through that door over there I recognized you as the man whose help I need here and now.'

'I may not want to help you,' the taciturn Jorje Katz pointed out as he downed his drink.

'With no wish to be offensive, what with civilization heading west faster than any wagon train ever did, I would suggest that as you are one of a dying breed you can't afford to be choosy.'

'I have always been what I want to be, and I don't intend to change right now.'

'Nevertheless, it's a right dreary night out there, raining heavily. I own several properties in town including the Stageline Hotel. Doubtless you could use a comfortable bed tonight,' Cusick said temptingly.

'Tonight's no different to other nights when my bedroll and slicker have kept me warm and dry, Cusick.'

Shaking his head slowly in amusement, Cusick said, 'But on those nights you didn't wake the next morning to the kind of money I'm about to offer you. I'll be paying you fighting wages.'

'What you want of me is more important to me than your money, Cusick.'

'It's all legal and above board,' Cusick assured him. 'We won't discuss it here. Come to my office tomorrow morning. You'll find it right opposite to the county jail. In the meantime I have business to attend to, but you stay here for as long as you wish. Drinks are on the house. I also own this place. Stable your horse at Al Petain's place just across the street from here. Tell Al that I will pick up the tab. I'll let Aretha Ryland who runs the hotel know that you are to have an evening meal, a room, and breakfast in the morning at my expense.'

'You could be wasting a whole heap of dollars.'

'That is a risk I'm prepared to take, Katz, as I am certain that we can work together,' Cusick confidently declared. 'Goodnight, my friend. *Hasta la vista.*'

Remaining detached from the people around him, Katz stayed for two further drinks. Carmencita, the girl who had earlier made a direct approach, hovered nearby. Plainly hurt by a scathing look from him, she turned and hurried away. Emptying his glass, he made his way to the door at a leisurely pace.

*

Originally from Philadelphia, Bartholomew Cusick had, since he was just twenty years old been driven by two compatible obsessions: money and politics. Being a charming, good-looking man who was cunning and had been born without a conscience, he considered himself competent to succeed in both of his ambitions. In pursuit of the former he had opened a gambling house in Santa Fe while educating himself in politics by mingling with the town's hierarchy among his clientele.

Always aware that he lacked what it takes to be a hard man, he had avoided injury or death in a business that was a magnet for violence by paying others to do his fighting for him.

Early in his career he had learned an important lesson the hard way. This was that meddling in politics before becoming wealthy seriously interfered with making money, and drastically stunted the rise to public office. You needed to be well heeled, reinforced with the power that comes with riches, before entering the political scene. So he had concentrated on business, purchasing a river boat and making it immensely popular with those seeking entertainment, and others, the majority, who were desperate to expand their prosperity through gambling. By the prudent selection of staff who were clever thieves such as he was, he ensured that the only winner on the *Lady Lolita*, the name he had given his river boat in honour of the part Mexican mother he had never known, would be Bartholomew Cusick.

Twenty years later he had arrived in Singing River. Wealthy and many times more unscrupulous, he was ready to launch himself into politics big time. Gaining control of local finance by establishing the Singing River Bank, he spent countless long hours currying favour with the town's rich and influential. He was now in the running to be Mayor of Singing River. With the election only a day away, he was strongly supported by people who were as ruthless as he was and who appreciated his stratagem of the subtle exploitation of the many for the benefit of the few. The threat to his being elected came from a clique of people that included ranchers in the district who were determined that his rival, 'Honest' Meredith Harland, the town's one and only lawyer, would become mayor.

Given publicity by Jeremiah Sutton, the proprietor of the town's newspaper *The River News*, the Harland faction was gaining strength, trading on criticism of the blatantly obvious alliance between the sheriff's office and Cusick. They emphasized that this was just one of the instances that proved that to elect Cusick would be to the detriment of all God-fearing, honest citizens. But Cusick was now confident he had found a way that evening to ensure victory.

His most dangerous enemy among the opposition was Clement Foy, the owner of the Six Bar Six ranch. Though a man who publicly spouted warnings of hell and damnation, Foy employed Sil Sontanna as range boss on his vast spread. A fast gun and ruthless killer, Sontanna had iron control over a thuggish assembly of former rustlers, outlaws and hired guns. Though acting as cowboys, none of them were reformed characters, but men for whom opportunities in their former unlawful ways of life were shrinking as real law enforcement came west. They terrorized the town on pay nights when they rode in to 'see the elephant' as they termed their wild celebrations.

If, as was certain to happen, Clement Foy brought his men into town on election day it would be a disaster. They would arrive at the polling place late in the day and destroy the majority of the votes for Bartholomew Cusick. Cusick had full control over Sheriff Ike Rownton and his deputies, but they wouldn't risk going up against Sontanna and his gang. Meredith Harland could walk straight in to climb into the mayor's chair. The obese Judge Handley, a big fish in Cusick's pool of corruption, held the power to rectify abuse of the election after the event, but not the courage to confront rancher Foy and his vicious gang in doing so.

Harland was perhaps worthy of the assumed name 'Honest' but he was no hero. Within weeks Clement Foy would be running him, and subsequently the whole district. Cusick was determined that that wouldn't happen. Having once seen Jorje Katz in action, a sight so fantastic that he had never forgotten one minute of it, he regarded Katz as his ace-in-the-hole. It would be a case of twenty or more against one, but that one would be the outstanding gunman Jorje Katz.

Going out into the dark, wet night, fortified by the thought of spending the coming hours under a roof after weeks of sleeping in the open, Katz was further pleased to discover that the exterior of the Stageline Hotel was impressive. The set-up at the Goldliner Saloon had prepared him to find himself in a disorderly house but the interior of the hotel exceeded his expectations. A wide, majestic and splendidly carpeted staircase swept up from a hall that was as tastefully furnished as the best private houses in the cities he had known.

Another pleasant surprise for him was Aretha Ryland. Expecting the hotel manageress to be of the standard of the women in Cusick's saloon, he had difficulty in concealing his astonishment when meeting her. An elegant lady wearing a tight-waisted green velvet jacket over a billowing skirt of golden braid, her fair hair was stylishly piled high, and her compelling blue eyes underscored the refined beauty of her face.

'Good evening, and welcome,' she warmly greeted him. 'As Bart Cusick's special guest you shall have the best room in the house. I will have Miguel show you up. Do you have luggage?'

'I've never stopped anywhere long enough to collect belongings, ma'am.'

'I like that answer,' she said, gesturing to the open door of a dining room where miners and ranchers sat among fat-bellied drummers avidly discussing orders received that day, and the hoped for orders of the morrow as they ate. 'You will gather that interesting conversation is thin on the ground where my usual guests are concerned.'

Further conversation between them was forestalled by the arrival of a young Mexican man clad in a blue uniform. Katz was shown to a luxuriously furnished, spacious room. In a curtained-off corner there was a large, gold-rimmed bathtub. Seeing him glance at the tub, the Mexican asked if he wished to bathe.

'I will bring you hot water, sir,' the Mexican said when Katz replied with an assenting nod.

Half an hour later Katz, bathed, shaved, and feeling good, was enjoying an excellent meal in the hotel dining room. Seduced by unaccustomed comforts and appetizing food he had, with just a few reservations, decided to work for Cusick. He had finished eating when Aretha Ryland made her graceful way toward his table carrying a bottle and two glasses. She paused hesitantly, looking at him without speaking, as he stood up from his chair.

Then she inquired indecisively. 'Am I intruding?'

'Not at all,' he assured her, reaching out to pull a chair across from another table.

Placing the glasses on the table she sat across from him. With a demure little smile she poured them both a drink, saying, 'Meeting you reminded me that there is a world outside of Singing River. I thought that if you could spare time to talk I could sample real life again, albeit second hand.'

'I wouldn't say that there is much real about my life, ma'am.'

'You are too modest,' she began. She indicated with a nod the gunbelt and holstered gun draped over the back of his chair. 'That, and the fact that you have purposely chosen a seat in a corner facing the door is something I find to be quite exciting here in Dullsville. May I call you Jorje?'

'Of course.'

'You will know that I am Aretha.'

'The Greek meaning of Aretha is virtue,' Katz mentioned conversationally.

'I have tried to forget that ever since I ceased being virtuous,' she joked. 'But I have a high regard for your wide knowledge. You really are an uncommonness in Singing River. Bart Cusick is absolutely enthralled by you. In normal circumstances there is nothing to be proud of in having Cusick praise you. It usually means no more than that you are a dishonest person.'

'It wouldn't seem that you hold Cusick in very high esteem, Aretha.'

'Quite the opposite actually.'

'Even though he owns this place?'

'It's because he owns this place that once was mine,' she replied vehemently. 'How long ago was that? A day? A year? A lifetime? I don't really know now. I find it too painful to look back, and I'm afraid to look forward into a bleak future. I just live for the present, if you can call it living. It's a long story that I will tell you at some time, if you are interested.'

'I am interested,' Katz assured her before sympathizing. 'You seem very sad.'

'I am sorry to burden you with my problems,' she apologized, reaching for the bottle to refill their glasses. 'Let us drink up and talk about pleasant things. Tell me all about that great big world out there.'

'The kind of world that I live in wouldn't be of much interest to you, Aretha.'

'You live dangerously, and life is never as exhilarating as when it could be taken away at any moment,' she argued. 'What you have experienced in life has imparted something special in you, something exciting that is tangible. Listen to me, prattling away like a silly woman. You must find me to be irritating.'

Giving her a reassuring smile, Katz said. 'I do find it strange that a poised lady such as you would be interested in the lower aspects of life.'

'Real life, that is what interests me, Jorje,' she enthusiastically informed him, refilling their glasses once more and settling back expectantly in her chair.

'Come in and sit down, Jorje. You are just the man I want to see,' Cusick rose from his chair smiling when Katz walked into his office the next morning. He indicated a man wearing a silver star who was beside him at the table. 'This is Ike, Sheriff Ike Rownton.'

The sheriff, a man of around Katz's own age, came up on to his feet and held out his right hand. The sheriff looked the part, wearing crossed gunbelts and a holstered revolver at both hips. Yet Katz instinctively recognized that Rownton had faced one showdown too many. It was plain that his nerve had gone.

Ignoring the proffered hand, Katz responded to the introduction with a curt nod and took a seat. Perhaps slightly influenced by Aretha Ryland's part-story of last evening, he mistrusted the over-friendly Cusick. But the death of Jasper Coker had left him destitute, robbing him of a planned future.

'You won't have been in town long enough to learn that we have an election for mayor here,' Cusick surmised.

'I haven't heard.'

'I am running for mayor.'

'I haven't heard that, either.'

Settling in his chair, elbows on the table, fingers laced under his chin, Cusick spoke earnestly. 'Unfortunately, this isn't a straightforward political issue. I need your help.'

'I have no knowledge of this sort of thing, so I don't see how I can help you, Cusick.'

'The kind of assistance I am willing to pay you handsomely for is not counting votes, but to ensure there are votes to count,' Cusick explained. 'There is a rancher named Clement Foy who is determined to have my rival elected.'

'I am, or I was, a gunfighter, not a bushwhacker, Cusick.'

'You misunderstand me,' Cusick said, hiding his annoyance behind an oily smile. 'I don't want you to kill Foy. He employs a bunch of renegades headed by a desperado by the name of Sil Sontanna. Sure as shooting tomorrow, Sontanna and his band of outlaws will ride into Singing River and wreck the polling place, destroying most of the votes for me in the process.'

'You have a sheriff to prevent that happening,' Katz remarked as he indicated Rownton with a sideways tilt of his head.

'Very true, very true. But as luck would have it Ike will be out of town on polling day, tending to other important business.'

'That sure must be important business,' Katz sarcastically

commented, rewarded by the sight of the sheriff ashamedly shifting in his chair and concentrating on staring out of the office window.

On this occasion Cusick was incapable of concealing his irritation. 'My reason for asking you here is a serious one, Katz, it is not to pass judgment on others present. If you do the job for me tomorrow in the manner in which I well know you are capable, then I will offer you permanent work. Believe me, there are many in town who would give their right arm to be on my payroll.'

'But not many prepared to give their lives, is my guess,' Katz commented. 'I kind of get the picture of what you want for me on voting day, but give me a rundown on it, Cusick.'

'I want you to be outside the polling place and prevent Sontanna and his men from entering.'

'How many do you anticipate?'

'Anything up to twenty, possibly one or two more.'

'I'm not surprised that the sheriff will be out of town that day.'

Aggravated once again, Cusick snapped, 'All you need to say is whether or not you will take on the task.'

'Depends on what you are going to pay me.'

Opening a drawer in his desk, Cusick took out a stuffed envelope and tossed it on to the desk in front of Katz. 'There's fifty dollars up front, Katz. When you have done what you have to do successfully, there will be another fifty for you, together with regular employment if you want it.'

'If I'm alive to accept the second fifty, then we can discuss me working for you,' Katz proposed.

'That's fine with me. Your free accommodation at the hotel is part and parcel of the deal we have struck.'

'Right. When is the big event?' Katz asked, as he got to his feet.

'Tomorrow,' Cusick replied as he stood up to gratefully shake Katz by the hand.

Late that evening Katz was leaning with both elbows on the bar of the Goldliner Saloon when he was joined by Carmencita the Mexican girl. In her slightly accented tone she inquired, 'Will I get my drink now, stranger?'

Remaining silent, Katz signalled to the bartender and pointed to the girl, who moved closer to him, waiting while the barkeep poured her drink. Then she lifted the glass as if about to thank him when shouting and laughing suddenly filled the saloon, so loud that it echoed from the balcony at the far end as a crowd of at least a dozen men made a stampede-like entrance. A noticeable air of menace came in with them.

Still holding her glass high Carmencita gave a brief, whimsical smile and instead of expressing her thanks, satirically toasted him, '*Vaya con Dios.*'

Swiftly interpreting her message that the arrival of the noisy gang would mean he would soon be leaving, he said, 'I guess these are Sontanna's men.'

'You guess right.'

'Which one is Sontanna?' Katz asked Carmencita without looking at the men who were now at the bar demanding drinks.

'He is not here. But you will know when he does arrive,' she warned him dramatically.

Someone started singing 'Oh! Susanna' and the others joined in with gusto. It was a discordant choir that grated on Katz, who waited an eternity for it to subside so as to hear what Carmencita was saying.

'Are you working for Bart Cusick now?' she asked.

'Maybe,' he replied as he became conscious of the nearest

of the Sontanna men studying him.

'Then you aren't going to find any friends among this lot,' she informed him.

'It's safer to be without friends, Carmencita.'

'That doesn't apply in Singing River. You need to have at least one good friend in this town, and you couldn't get a better one than me.'

'Why do you say that?'

'Because if you are involved with Cusick you will need someone who knows what is going on around here, and I am that someone. Even the most cautious of men talk indiscreetly when they have drink taken and I have trained myself to be a good listener.'

'Then it's possible that we—' Katz began before being interrupted by the Foy man who had been staring.

'A friendly word of advice, stranger. Carmencita is Sil Sontanna's woman.'

'Watch him. It's Jim Curran, a right troublemaker,' Carmencita cautioned Katz before hissing at the man, 'I'm nobody's woman.'

'You heard her,' Katz said calmly, with both elbows remaining on the bar and without turning his head. 'She's nobody's woman.'

'You won't be so gosh-darned high-falutin' when Sontanna gets here,' the man warned Katz.

'Stick around until he arrives and you'll find out,' Katz suggested.

Turning to beckon to his companions, the aggressive man took one step back as he challenged Katz to face him. 'I ain't never yet shot a man in the back.'

'You surprise me,' Katz rejoined, not moving from his position leaning on the bar.

This reply caused someone in the crowd to laugh.

Infuriated at being mocked, the Foy man went for his gun. Making no attempt at firing it, he gripped the Colt .45 peacemaker by the barrel intent on giving Katz a pistol whipping, aiming the butt at the back of Katz's head.

Acting intuitively, astonishing the onlookers, Katz pushed Carmencita out of harm's way with one arm while swinging the other arm back to smash the elbow into Curran's face. Hurtling backwards Curran crashed into a table, toppling it and several chairs. The crashing of tables against the wooden floor, together with the sound of glasses smashing was a miniature explosion. Curran slammed onto the floor on his back, where he lay unconscious with blood pouring thickly from his nose and mouth.

Then there was total quiet. The first noise to follow was the footfalls of someone coming into the saloon. Every eye in the place was dragged away from the distressed man on the floor to take in the newcomer. It was a lean man with a gaunt face, who moved with a lithe grace to stand and look down at Curran. Face expressionless, he briefly studied the body before looking up questioningly at the group of now silent men who stood motionless at the bar. One of them pointed to Katz who stood relaxed with his back against the bar.

Cold anger on his hard face, the lean man walked across the saloon to stand facing Katz at a distance of some ten feet.

TWO

'I am Sil Sontanna,' the man announced, keeping his gaze on Katz while pointing behind himself. 'That man lying there is both an employee and a buddy of mine.'

'Curran asked for what he got,' Carmencita volunteered herself as a witness.

'The word of a mouthy saloon g'hal don't mean nothing,' Sontanna snarled at her before warning Katz. 'I'm not the kind of *hombre* who'd let someone do that to one of my men and get away with it.'

Still leaning, relaxed, with his back against the bar, Katz nodded. 'Go ahead, make your play.'

'That's not how it's going to be,' Sontanna said, shaking his head. 'I do everything by my rules. Sooner or later we will meet again. Maybe it will be the next time we meet, maybe not. Whatever, from the minute you walk out of here tonight you'll be constantly looking over your shoulder worrying about when I will make my move.'

'That will work both ways,' Katz cautioned.

'Never,' Sontanna disputed. 'No man can match Sil Sontanna on the draw.'

Satisfied that he had forcefully made his point, Sontanna dismissively turned his back and walked away.

'What if he's right?' Carmencita asked worriedly.

'Then you had better let me buy you another drink while I am still able to.'

'You are a difficult man to read,' a perplexed Carmencita complained. 'Does nothing worry you?'

'Right now I am concerned for you,' Katz admitted. 'You being Sontanna's woman, he isn't going to be happy about you being with me. I don't like leaving you here alone.'

With a tight little smile she raised a shapely leg and pointed to the knife in her garter saying. 'I am not alone.'

Impressed by her tough demeanour, Katz's attention was drawn to a loud rattling, coughing sound. He looked to where Curran, his face a dark purple, lay on his back choking on his own blood. Two of his companions quickly crouched to turn him onto his face. In a gurgling explosion, Curran spewed out the blood he had swallowed since Katz had mashed his nose and mouth. Standing close, watching what had obviously been Curran's life being saved, Sontanna turned his head to glower at Katz.

'Even so, I would prefer it if you stayed close to me until Sontanna and his border ruffians leave here,' Katz explained to Carmencita.

'Nothing could please me more,' she assured him.

It was late and her staff, with the exception of Miguel who was behind the reception desk, had completed their tasks and retired to their quarters. Aretha Ryland was tired. very tired, but contradictorily restless. She paced slowly around the hotel's vestibule.

Old Doc Walpole, a bachelor who was never in a hurry to go home after his regular evening meal at the hotel, was half-dozing in an armchair. Occasionally he would startle her by muttering a few words. In the main it was medical terms that meant nothing to her. Aware that she should politely usher the short, plump, somewhat shambling doctor to the door, and head for her room, she could not bring herself to do so.

She well knew the reason for her dilemma with regard to retiring for the night. It was because she couldn't get Jorje Katz out of her mind. In some strange way he had changed her life for the better simply by walking into the hotel.

Things had been good when she had first arrived in Singing River. She had invested her savings from a successful career back East as an actress, in starting up as an hotelier by having a grand building constructed in the style of New York theatres. In keeping with the design, she had named it the Broadway Hotel. The town had been young and enthusiastic at that time, and her business had progressed steadily if not spectacularly. Everything about her hotel enterprise had begun to go downwards soon after Bartholomew Cusick had appeared in the town.

First establishing the Singing River Bank, the flamboyant Cusick had then opened a large general store, followed by the soon to become notorious Goldliner Saloon. When his next venture had been a hotel, she had not been concerned. Named the Rest and Welcome, it had none of the class of her establishment; therefore she didn't regard it as a threat, not until she learned that his charges undercut hers to such an extent that his hotel must have been running at a loss. It wasn't until her trade had diminished alarmingly that she realized he had run it at a loss deliberately to force her out of business.

A few months later she had been in severe financial difficulties. Having starred in the long-running Civil War drama *Shenandoah*, she had briefly considered returning to New York and the stage, but was aware that too many years had probably gone by for her to succeed in reviving her former vocation. She recognized that any chance for her to survive lay right here in Singing River. Hating every minute of it, she had been forced to ask at Cusick's bank for a substantial loan.

Dealing personally with her application, Cusick had pointed out that for a loan of the size she required her premises would not provide sufficient collateral. This bad news determined that she was left with no option but to sell her business. The only prospective buyer was Cusick, whose offer was no more than a pittance. With no alternative, but with an insipient hatred of Cusick that had ever since accrued, she had accepted his offer. Renaming the Broadway the Stageline Hotel, Cusick closed his own excuse for a hotel, and had, surprisingly, kept her on as manageress. However, not a day had since passed without him at least once reminding her subtly of the power he had over her.

In recent months she had been considering leaving Singing River and using the small amount of money Cusick had paid for her hotel to start a similar, but more modest, business elsewhere. But meeting Jorje Katz had changed her mind. For a reason that she couldn't fathom, Katz had given her hope.

Hope for what, she didn't know. Right now, as Doc Walpole stirred in his chair, she decided her long wait was pointless. Jorje Katz was not going to come back to the hotel that night.

As if reading her mind, Doc Walpole, who was far from the bumbling old fool people took him to be, called across to her. 'Yours is a lost cause, my dear Aretha. It wouldn't seem that Lothario will return to you tonight.'

Her acting career suggested to her that the old man was referring to a Shakespearean lover. Needing further qualification, she asked. 'Who are you talking about, Doc?'

'That handsome fellow you sat talking with at dinner,' the old physician said as he folded the newspaper he had been reading and donned his hat. 'The two of you were a perfect match.'

'Not for long apparently,' she grumpily remarked.

'*Nil Desperandum*, Aretha,' he consoled her. 'I'll bid you goodnight, my dear. Get yourself to bed. Things will look much brighter in the morning.'

Walking with him to the door, she said. 'There's little chance of that happening in Singing River.'

She stood at the door for a few minutes with the doctor. Two men who knew him exchanged greetings as they walked by.

A compassionate man, the doctor tried to help her by asking them, 'Have you been in the Goldliner?'

'Where else?' one of them replied with a question of his own.

'Did you happen to notice a stranger there?'

'Couldn't not have done so if you are referring to a gunfighter named Katz.'

'That's the man,' Doc Walpole confirmed, earning Aretha's gratitude.

'I'd avoid him if I was you, Doc,' the youngest of the two men advised. 'He's not a man to tangle with.'

'Not unless your name is Carmencita,' the other man laughed.

'What does that mean?' Walpole inquired.

Gesturing towards the saloon, still chuckling the man said. 'She's in there with him now.'

Saddened by this unexpected information, the old doctor sympathetically squeezed Aretha's arm then made a hurried getaway by waddling off towards his home.

It was so late that with Walpole and the two men gone the street was deserted. Stepping outside, an unhappy Aretha looked to see that the Naphtha lights outside of the Goldliner Saloon had been doused and the place was in complete darkness.

Hoping against hope to see Jorje Katz walking in her direction, she was bitterly disappointed. Turning, she went back in and closed the door, mourning the loss of her short-lived dream.

Disappointment gripped like an ice hand in her stomach, freezing all emotion and all desire for life that had been returning to her in the charismatic presence of this gunfighter.

'They are coming! They are coming!' the boy Cusick had stationed on the perimeter of town to watch for Clement Foy's men, cried out the warning over and over again as he ran to the polling place.

Bored by a long and uneventful day so far, Katz welcomed the news as he rested against the hitching rail outside of the church hall that was serving as an election station. Apart from the dragging hours it hadn't been a good day for him. Having always been self-sufficient, it had shocked him to discover that Aretha's aloofness towards him at breakfast in the hotel had hurt him. He guessed the reason for it was the hours he had spent with Carmencita last night. But he didn't regret that. The saloon girl had deserved his protection, having bravely sided with him against Sontanna.

Now, first taking an anxious look out of the door, Cusick came out to make his way toward where Katz stood and ask. 'You heard what the kid said.'

'I heard.'

'You are prepared?'

'I'm ready.'

'You are taking on a tremendous task,' Cusick warned.

'That's what you are paying me for,' Katz reminded him as a group of riders some ten abreast in two rows came round the corner into the street and rode at a trot towards them. Katz advised, 'You'll be safer inside, Cusick.'

Ashen faced, Cusick said hoarsely. 'God, there's more than twenty of them!'

Turning on his heel he rushed back into the hall as Katz stepped out into the middle of the street to face the oncoming horsemen. At the centre of the front rank was Sil Sontanna riding beside a distinguished looking man with a grey goatee, wearing a white suit and a white Stetson. The group reined up when Katz held up both hands, palms towards them.

'Fan out across the street in a single line,' he ordered them.

Sontanna turned his head to look at his boss who nodded, and Sontanna called. 'String out in one line, boys.'

Katz kept a watchful eye on the riders as they made the manoeuvre.

'We haven't met,' the white-suited man said cordially. 'I take it that you are Jorje Katz.'

'That's right. I guess you are Clement Foy?'

'That is correct. I am given to understand that you have acquired a most impressive reputation as a gunfighter, Katz. However, permit me to explain that neither I nor any one of my men has any quarrel with you. I am here on a peaceful mission to cast my vote in a democratic election.'

'That's fine. You can dismount and go inside, but each and every one of your men must remain in the saddle.'

'I should explain, Katz, that through no fault of his own, a man who owns a vast spread such as the Six Bar Six gains enemies. That being so, I always make it a rule to have my foreman accompany me in all public places.'

With a negative shake of his head, Katz informed him. 'Then you have just met your first exception to that rule. Sontanna stays where he is.'

Sontanna muttered something that Katz couldn't catch, but he could see that Foy's façade of amiability had considerably faded as he asked, 'Might I inquire on whose authority you are issuing orders to respectable citizens going about their lawful business?'

'Judge Colt,' Katz answered, patting his holstered revolver. 'I am not preventing you from voting. Tell your men to remain mounted, and then get off your horse.'

Openly showing his annoyance now, Foy dismounted and kept well away from Katz as he headed for the door of the polling place. Not taking his eyes off the horsemen, Katz beckoned with his left hand for Foy to come to him. Halting close to him, Foy protested as Katz reached out with his left hand to undo his jacket and pluck a derringer one-shot pistol from Foy's waistband.

'You won't need this parlour gun to cast your vote. Go ahead now,' Katz said, throwing the small pistol into the dust at the side of the road.

'I carried that weapon solely for personal protection,' Foy tetchily told him.

'You are free to pick it up out of the dirt when you come out of the polling place,' Katz affirmed, earning himself a baleful glare in return.

As Foy went in through the door of the building, Sontanna smiled a mirthless smile and said, 'This is our second meeting, Katz. Could this be the time I get even?'

'The choice is yours, Sontanna,' Katz invited.

'If I draw and by some miracle you get lucky, Katz, then there's twenty men here who will gun you down.'

'That won't be much consolation to you,' Katz observed, 'seeing as you will be lying dead in the dirt with a bullet in your heart.'

The line-up of horses was constantly moving restlessly, an aspect of the situation that forced Katz to be extra watchful. He was alerted by a movement of a horse that had one rider moving slightly to the rear so that he was partly concealed by the horsemen between him and Katz. Sontanna had begun speaking once more but Katz's suspicions regarding the partially hidden rider held his attention.

Taking a small step to his left, a slight movement in the line of horses allowed him to see that the rider was unaware that he had lost a small part of his concealment. No more than a boy, he was slowly and furtively pulling his gun from its holster.

With no time to take the rider's youth into consideration, Katz drew and fired. His bullet knocked the boy violently backwards. Had his foot not been caught in one stirrup he would have instantly hit the ground. There was pandemonium for a moment as the frightened horses close to the horse with the boy hanging by his right foot, made it difficult for their riders to control them.

Partly obscured by other riders, with only his head and shoulders as a target, another horseman started to draw his revolver. But the eagle-eyed Katz read the signs and instantly released a shot. His bullet hit the would-be shootist in the head. A fountain of blood erupted from the man's skull before he fell out of the saddle.

'What is the shooting about?' Foy yelled as he came running out of the polling place.

'He's killed the boy, Dude Frampton, and Skiff Hemingway,' Sontanna reported.

Hurrying over to look down at the dead boy who now lay crumpled in the dust, and then the other man Katz had shot, Foy turned to Katz. 'You have caused yourself a lot of trouble here, Katz.'

'Both the boy and the other guy drew on me first, Foy. If you want to argue about that, then make a complaint to Sheriff Rownton,' Katz responded. 'You have voted, which is what you came into town to do. I want no further trouble. So pick up your dead and ride out of town with your men.'

On Foy's instructions, three men picked up the two

bodies, laid them across their saddles and secured them with ropes. Foy looked to Sontanna for his opinion on what their next move should be but his range boss was concentrating on organizing the retreat that Katz had ordered. Foy angrily mounted up and reined his horse around to ride through his line of riders and head off up the street. His men quickly followed.

With the danger over, Cusick took one tentative step out of the church hall to remark to Katz. 'You put the skids under them, Jorje, that sure is certain. What's the chances of them coming back?'

'They'll be back, but not today,' Katz assured him. 'Your election is safe. When they do come it will be for me.'

'Call in at my office later and pick up your money. You've earned it.'

Watching Cusick go back inside, Katz considered that he had more than earned his money. He had sown a wind today that would ensure he would soon be hit by a whirlwind that would make a hundred dollars poor compensation.

Dinner at the Six Bar Six ranch house that evening began in silence. Foy sat at the head of a huge table, with his wife at the opposite end and his son sitting to his right. An elderly Arapaho woman waited on them.

Diminished by years of marriage to her strictly religious but domineering husband, Agnes Foy had long ago adopted a don't-speak-unless-you-are-spoken-to strategy. Abraham, their 18-year-old son, did his best to follow her way of maintaining peace in the household, yet youthful exuberance sometimes had him stray from the narrow path of behaviour laid down by his father. One of those occasions was about to occur.

'What difference can it make to us that Bartholomew

Cusick has been elected as mayor, Father?' Abraham, an intellectual rather than a physical young man, questioned.

'The general answer to that would take quite some time to explain, son,' Clement Foy replied in a controlled tone that worried his wife who knew how strongly he felt on the subject. She listened intently, waiting for the fire and brimstone facet of his personality to erupt as he continued. 'Though now undoubtedly destined to be a greater threat in the future, Cusick is not the immediate problem. Today we lost Dude Frampton, a boy of about the same age as yourself, and Skiff Hemingway, as good a man as ever there was. That is down to a gunfighter by the name of Jorje Katz. That man is our priority.'

'What will that entail, Clem?' Agnes anxiously inquired, as fearful of having asked the question as she was of the answer that would be forthcoming.

'Ultimately Katz's fate must rightfully be left to Sil. In the meantime I will have a word with Jake, Ron and Harold.'

'Give him a beating!' Abraham exclaimed, with too much excitement for his mother's comfort, as he recognized the names of three powerfully built Six Bar Six hands. The trio were brutes who mistreated without compunction both animals and human beings.

'Maybe that is the form in which Katz should initially be punished,' Foy replied without committing himself.

'Then Sil will get him,' Abraham contentedly surmised. 'Will Sil then get Cusick, Father?'

Foy reprimanded him. 'We do neither sponsor nor condone killing, son. In the case of Katz it will be justice. But Bartholomew Cusick is a politician who is staking his claim to Singing River by stealth. We shall confront and defeat him by the same method.'

'Can he be beaten, Clem?' Agnes queried. Making a small

'no more' gesture with her hand as the Arapaho woman approached with a coffee pot, she went on, 'He is a clever man.'

'Devious is a description I would use rather than clever, Agnes,' Foy corrected her, 'and deviousness, in the way of all wickedness, is vulnerable to opposition from all right-thinking people.'

'You said earlier that Jorje Katz is a lightning fast gunfighter. Would you consider him to be vulnerable to anything, even Sil Sontanna, Father?' Abraham inquired in a bland way that he hoped would elicit a meaningful answer without bringing his father's wrath down upon him.

Deep in thought for a long time as he considered this question, Clement then gave his son a deliberately evasive reply. 'I don't believe that is something that should be discussed at the dinner table, Abraham. Especially with your mother present.'

Jorje Katz reined up his magnificent black stallion on the brow of a hill. Now distanced from Singing River he found a much-needed feeling of peace settling on him, something he hadn't experienced since his arrival in that town. Make the most of it, he morosely told himself as he looked down a wooded slope that swept to where a homestead huddled cosily in a flat area. Even from a remote viewing point he could see livestock and pick out sections of cultivated land.

It was a sight that impressed on him the grim task that lay immediately ahead. When Foy and his men had left town he had collected his second fifty dollars from Cusick, who had displayed an eagerness to secure his services on a permanent basis. Though far from impressed by his experiences of Singing River up to that point, common sense had told him that it was necessary for him to earn a worthwhile sum of money before moving on. Yet this mission repulsed him. What happened in the immediate future would have him decide if he wanted to continue in the employ of Cusick, a man he detested.

Giving him directions to get to the homestead he was now looking down on, the new Mayor of Singing River had explained irately, 'That cussed nester out there is well behind with repayments on a loan and he doesn't care a hooter. Get out there and teach him an all-fired lesson, Jorje. He isn't likely to have a dime to his name, so threaten the coot that you'll take whatever he owns that is dear to him, keeping his hovel of a cabin in reserve as the final threat.'

Sitting in the saddle with that cabin in view, smoke rising from its chimney, Katz, who was no stranger to hard times, had no stomach for what he would be facing when he reached the bottom of the slope.

Unable to think of an alternative in his present circumstances, he pulled in a deep breath, nudged the stallion lightly in the flanks with his spurs, and moved on.

Bartholomew Cusick had slipped away from the celebratory lunch in his mayoral honour that was taking place in the Stageline Hotel to join Aretha in reception. Knowing what to expect she had ledgers in which she had entered the hotel's income and outgoings for the past few days open on the desk for him to avidly peruse.

Though this was not an out of the ordinary spontaneous audit on the part of the money-obsessed Cusick, Aretha was astonished that such a vain man would consider leaving a gathering of adoring followers to count a relatively small amount of dollars when he could be standing among sycophants eager to continuously shower him with praise.

Running a forefinger slowly down each column, his lips

moved as he silently added up each entry and checked each total he reached with the figures entered at the bottom of the column, to the annoyance of Aretha.

'That's fine,' he said, at last closing the books, quickly adding, 'However, the volume of business recorded here in no way reflects the potential of this hotel. There is still room for improvement.'

'I don't see where,' Aretha disputed, proud of the steady increase she had created in the volume of business.

'We'll discuss that issue at a later date, Aretha. One saving that can be made instantly is moving Jorje Katz to one of the cheaper rooms. He is in my employment now and will be paying to stay here at the hotel. The same goes for whatever he consumes in the dining room. Cash in hand, of course, the same as anyone we don't know well.'

'Have you informed him of this?' she inquired, purely out of interest as she had already decided what the answer would be.

'I haven't had the opportunity to tell him, Aretha.'

'But you will be doing so?'

'There is no reason for me to do so,' Cusick replied impatiently. 'Neither am I required to. There is nothing special about Jorje Katz, who is no more than another person in my employ. That applies also to you, who I appointed as manageress of this hotel. Being in that position it is you who must explain the change and the reason for the change in his arrangements here.'

Used to having him talk down to her in this way, Aretha was sickened by his change of attitude towards Katz now that he had got what he wanted from him; she was on the verge of remonstrating with Cusick on the subject when one of his flunkeys came out of the dining room.

'Meredith Harland is about to make his speech conceding

defeat and congratulating you, Mayor Cusick.'

'I'll be right there, Cecil.'

Cusick walked away with his head high. His avarice satisfied, he was now ready to feed his vanity. Watching him go, Aretha seethed with pent up anger.

Leaning over in the saddle to reach down and open the wooden gate, Katz rode into the small fenced enclosure, reaching down again to close the gate behind him. The homestead was obviously well managed and the livestock well cared for. It had none of the appearance of neglect that usually went with an unpaid debt to a bank. Dismounting, he was hitching his horse some distance from the cabin when a shout had him turn. A young man was standing in the cabin doorway levelling a shotgun at him.

'Whoever you are, whatever you want here, just mount up and ride away, mister,' the dark-skinned man ordered.

'Are you Joel Edwards?' Katz asked.

'It ain't no never mind what my name is. Just mount up and light out of here mighty fast.'

Not making any move to suggest that he was about to obey the order he had been given, Katz said. 'I'm not about to do that. I work for Bartholomew Cusick, and I am here on his business.'

'That tells me all I need to know about you,' the man snarled, making a little threatening jerk with the shotgun. 'All the more reason for you to get off my property.'

'You are not doing yourself any favours—' Katz began, breaking off in mid-sentence when the sudden sound of a child crying loudly in distress came through the open door of the cabin.

Then a woman screamed. 'Joel! Come in here QUICKLY!'

THREE

Turning his back on Katz, the young man propped his shotgun against the doorjamb and rushed into the cabin. Hesitating for a split second, Katz went over and picked up the shotgun, breaking it to remove the cartridge. Placing the cartridge in his shirt pocket, he put the shotgun back against the jamb, then entered the cabin.

The interior was poorly illuminated by just one small window, but there was light enough for Katz to see a woman with fair hair bending over one side of a homemade cot, weeping and wringing her hands. The man named Joel was at the other side of the little bed applying a wet flannel to a child who Katz could hear was still crying but couldn't see.

Moving closer, expecting to see a baby, he was astonished to find himself looking at a girl whom he estimated was six or seven years of age. The child was sweating profusely to the extent that her father was fighting a losing battle against her temperature. Each time he took the cloth away to wring it out the girl's face and neck was soaked with sweat before he could recommence his ministrations.

Noticing for the first time that Katz had come into the cabin, Edwards continued tending to his daughter but his teeth gritted in rage as he commanded Katz, 'Get out of here. You are here to do Cusick's dirty work, and we have enough to worry about with Estelle's illness. We don't need people like you bothering us, so get out and be on your way.'

'Your little girl is very sick, so we shouldn't waste time by arguing between ourselves,' Katz commented calmly, not moving. 'She urgently needs help. Is there a doctor in Singing River?'

'Yes, Doc Walpole,' the woman dried her tears long to reply.

'That's no use to us, Heather,' Joel told her.

'Why not?' Katz inquired.

'It is none of your darn business,' Joel snapped.

'I want to help.'

'Tell him why, Joel, please,' Heather begged.

Giving her plea some thought as he continued nursing his daughter, Joel reluctantly muttered. 'The doc is a good man and an excellent doctor, but it used to cost us twenty-five dollars a year to have him tend all three of us. As you will know, otherwise you wouldn't be out here ready to cause us trouble, things haven't been good and we haven't been able to afford that for the last four years or so.'

'Nevertheless,' Katz advised. 'Your little girl needs a doctor pronto.'

'What do you think is wrong with her?' an apprehensive Heather asked, plainly hoping for an encouraging reply.

Katz couldn't oblige. Having seen similar cases in the past he was fairly certain that it was cholera, a disease that could kill within hours. He had been in a town that had been hit by the dreadful scourge of the disease. The terrible ravages of this malady had brought death to many and terrororized countless others with the fear of death. He had seen the flesh of corpses disintegrate into a putrefied mass shortly after death. These weren't memories to share with the parents of a sick child.

Katz said. 'I don't know but she definitely needs urgent medical attention. There isn't time for me to ride into town and fetch the doctor back here. We need to make some kind of arrangement, and we need it fast. Do you have any kind of suitable transport, Joel?'

'Only an old buckboard,' Edwards answered helpfully, Katz's concern for the girl having convinced him that she really was in danger. 'It is serviceable, but hardly a proper means of taking a little girl as sick as Estelle is all the way into town.'

Katz expressed his opinion. 'All that's needed is a seat on which your wife can sit holding Estelle in her arms. Let us get her wrapped in blankets while you hitch up the buckboard. Then we'll be on our way to the doctor in town. Get moving now. Believe me, time is extremely important. I'll ride just ahead all the way.'

'We have no money to pay Doc Walpole,' Joel Edwards, losing the enthusiasm that Katz had generated in him, dismissed the idea hollowly.

'We will sort out the money situation when the time comes,' Katz brusquely argued. 'It is your daughter that we need to take care of now. There is no time to waste, Joel. Get the buckboard hitched up and we'll get moving.'

Meredith Harland's speech was unexpectedly critical of Mayor Cusick. It offended the majority of those present but delighted Aretha Ryland.

'Those of you who are expecting some kind of lick finger speech from me had better vamoose right now,' Harland, generally regarded as a weak man, began. 'It is customary for a defeated candidate to say the better man won. I am about to break from that tradition. The good people of Singing

River have been duped. They set out to elect themselves an upstanding citizen as mayor but got themselves a scallywag, a member of the codfish aristocracy prepared to ruthlessly exploit each and every one of us to make money for himself.'

There was an outbreak of booing and catcalls. Mayor Cusick sprang to his feet to shout abuse at Harland, but was pulled back to his seat by one of his advisers.

Eventually restoring order, Harland completed his condemnation of Cusick by offering a solution to what he saw as a disaster for the district. 'I ask you good citizens to follow me in my campaign to clear this monstrous situation from our town before it has the opportunity to ruin all of us.'

Getting to his feet once more, Cusick bellowed. 'Those who follow a cowardly coyote like Meredith Harland will find him a long way behind you when the going gets tough. I am the democratically elected mayor of Singing River. Attempt to oust me and you will be breaking the law.'

'What's that, Cusick, your kind of law where you have Sheriff Rownton jumping through hoops like an all-fired performing dawg?' someone shouted, the first sign of the tide of support turning against him.

This caused laughter that faded away when the intellectual Meredith Harland concluded his speech with a rallying call. 'I am not a man given to blasphemy but now, my dear friends, I am forced to put into words what you already have in your minds.' He raised his voice so that his words rang around the spacious dining room. 'No one of us can grant a son-of-a-bitch like Bartholomew Cusick the total freedom to control Singing River. I have no intention of doing so, and I rely on you all to join me.'

With a defiant glare at Cusick, Harland strode from the room to deafening applause and cheering that completely drowned out the almost hysterical, indignant yelling of Cusick.

*

Riding just ahead of the Edwards' buckboard just some five miles from Singing River, Katz entered a narrow gorge to find the way ahead blocked. Three men stood side-by-side in front of their horses. There was no way past them. Reining up, Katz stayed in the saddle, waiting. He was baffled as to why all three of the powerfully-built men were unarmed.

Spreading his hands wide to emphasize this fact, the man in the centre, the biggest of the three, spoke in a friendly manner. 'There's no call for gunplay, Katz. We are Six Bar Six men. Clement Foy sent us out to ask if we may have a word with you.'

'Say your piece and then move aside,' Katz said as the buckboard came into the gorge behind him and he waved a hand to have Joel Edwards stay back.

'Are these people in the buckboard anything to you?'

'You asked to speak to me, and I agreed. So quit asking questions or I'll be on my way.'

Smiling while he turned to indicate the narrowness of the gorge and the three horse, two men barricade, the man said, 'Seems to me like you don't have an option to move on.'

'I reckon as how I'm toting a six-gun and you three are unarmed, gives me that option,' Katz disagreed.

'From what I've heard you are too proud a man to take advantage of that. Now listen up. What we need to discuss with you is kinda private. I'm Ron Hillier, the spokesman, while this galoot on my left is Jake McCabe, and on my right is Harold Hay. They will stay right here while I walk over to talk to you if you will climb down from the saddle.'

Desperate to get the Edwards' daughter to the doctor, starkly aware of the consequences of any delay, Katz wanted to deal with whatever it was the three men represented swiftly and without violence. Dismounting, he stood in front of his horse waiting for Hillier.

Hiller approached to stand within a couple of feet of him to say. 'The problem is that you are heading the wrong way. Foy wants you to head away from town, and not to stop. If you ever was welcome in Singing River, then that welcome has run out.'

Katz realized that he had a serious problem. This trio of thugs were there to give him such a beating that he would be convinced that he must ride away from Singing River forever. How was he to handle the difficulty that he faced? Hillier had deliberately come close to make it easy to stop him if he went for his gun. He was figuring out the best move to make, if there was such a move to be made, when the sick girl's suffering had her suddenly cry out. It was a high pitched shriek that resounded repeatedly from the high walls of the gorge.

It was a sound that powerfully impressed the gravity of the child's condition on Katz who involuntarily turned his head in the direction of the buckboard. It was only for a split second, but Hiller used it to fell him with a terrifically hard rabbit punch. He fell heavily to the mesquite-covered floor of the gorge. Barely conscious and with no control over his limbs, he was vaguely aware of Hillier kicking him hard in the ribs. Then the other two men were dragging him to his feet. When he was being held upright a grinning Hillier first disarmed him and then smashed a vicious punch into his face.

Hearing the sound of boots scraping on wood and realizing that Joel Edwards was about to get down from the buckboard seat to help him, Katz shouted a warning. 'Stay where you are, Joel.'

He wasn't capable of saying anything else as with the other two men still holding him, Hillier swung his right arm to catch him another powerful blow to the side of his face.

Struggling to remain conscious, Katz knew that for him to take one more blow would mean that the tiny Estelle Edwards would die out here in the wilds. Thinking quickly, he came up with the only strategy open to him.

With the two men on either side keeping their hold on him, and Hillier relishing the power he had at that time by deliberately delaying as he prepared to throw another punch, Katz went into action. Gathering his strength, he thrust both his feet hard against the ground and lunged himself backwards at his stallion.

Panicked by the hard collision, the horse reared. Its front legs hit Katz in the back sending him forwards with such force that he slammed into Hillier, knocking him flat on his back, while the two men each side of him lost their grip.

Quick to take advantage of the situation, and immensely relieved to see that the fall had winded and temporarily immobilized Hillier, he turned to his left to see that one of the stallion's hoofs had smashed in the skull of the man who had been holding him on that side. The man on the right was unharmed and was coming at him in a rush. Standing his ground, Katz let the man come. Grabbing the lapels of his attacker's jacket, he pulled and let himself fall backwards, taking the man with him. Folding his legs up against his chest as his back hit the ground, Katz straightened his legs at the right moment so that his feet came against the man's stomach. Pushing hard with both legs he propelled the man in a somersault over his head.

On his feet, even as his assailant hit the ground, Katz ran to him. Eyes open wide and rolling in his head, the man lay on his back. With Hillier already unsteadily rising to his hands and knees, and with neither the time nor a reason to feel compassion, Katz stamped hard on the fallen man's throat, crushing his trachea. Hearing the death rattle issue from the man's mouth, he hurried to where Hillier had recovered sufficiently to get up into a squatting position with his back to Katz.

Arriving at a run behind Hillier, Katz kicked out with his right foot to strike him on the buttocks with the flat of his booted foot and send him face down on the ground. Without pausing Katz landed with both knees on Hillier's upper back. Reaching to cup his chin with both hands and increasing pressure with his knees as he pulled Hillier's head up. A wheezing Hillier begged. 'No! Please no!'

Pulling harder on the big man's chin, Katz ignored the plea that was the last Hillier would make until his neck snapped with a crack as loud as the report of a Sharp's heavy calliper rifle being fired.

Leaping up from the dead man, Katz put a foot in a stirrup and swung up into the saddle shouting to Joel Edwards. 'Bring the girl to me.'

Both Edwards and his wife were stunned by what they had just witnessed, and it took Joel a little while to fathom what was required of him; Edwards then got the message as his wife passed him their blanket-wrapped daughter. He ran to hand the child up to Katz.

'I am going to ride fast into town,' Katz informed Edwards as he took the girl. 'You follow me in. Rein up at the Stageline Hotel and ask for Aretha Ryland, the manageress. She will tell you where I have taken your daughter.'

Having delivered that message, Katz, who held the reins in one hand and cradled the child in the other arm, dug in the spurs and galloped away.

In his office, the walls of which were lined with bookcases packed with books of different sizes and covers of various colours, Meredith Harland sat behind a desk patiently awaiting a response from the three men standing across the desk from him.

'I'm with you all the way, Meredith,' Jeremiah Sutton the owner of the *Singing River News* pledged. 'I'll give the campaign you have outlined full support in the columns of my newspaper.'

The cautious Zak Horton, who ran the town's feed store, expressed his misgivings. 'It will take more than mere printed words for us to have an effect on the regime that Cusick will soon have in place. I predict that Clement Foy, the major opposition to him becoming mayor, will consider it prudent to throw in his lot with Cusick.'

'A case of if you can't lick 'em join 'em,' blacksmith Jem Fraser ironically commented before issuing a serious warning. 'Should those two unite there would be little point in attempting to oppose them. That gang of desperados that Foy employs will hold this whole town to ransom. We won't have a hope.'

'What about this Katz fellow?' Sutton asked.

'What about him?' Harland replied with a question of his own.

'Well, I understand that he is a force to be reckoned with, so it would be prudent to discover whose side he will be on.'

'He is working for Cusick,' Fraser said, 'so there is no reason to believe that will alter anytime in the future.'

'Perhaps if we get all the business folk together we could have the resources to hire our own gang of fighting men,' Zak Horton tentatively suggested.

Shocked by this, Jeremiah Sutton exclaimed, 'In this day and age of supposed enlightenment, I would view that as a retrograde step. We need to encourage Preacher Donne to come in with us. He would have nothing to do such an ungodly arrangement.'

'With no disrespect to the preacher,' Horton countered, 'he would doubtless suggest prayer as an alternative. Clement Foy is always telling anyone who will listen that he is a God-fearing man, and prayer sure ain't going to stop that big bug who's as mad as a peeled rattler when he don't get his own way.'

'I believe we should refrain at this stage from either ruling anything in or anything out,' Harland said in an effort to calm the small group. 'Our best plan is to contact everyone interested and then arrange a meeting where every possibility can be discussed and either agreed on or dismissed.'

The other three men all nodded in assent.

When Jorje Katz came in through the doors of the hotel in a rush, clasping the child to him, Aretha Ryland recoiled at the sight of his badly swollen and bruised face. 'What on earth has happened to you, Jorje?'

'That's of no account,' he breathlessly told her. 'This little girl is seriously ill. Can you tell me where the doctor's place is, Aretha?'

Concern on her face as she looked at the small blanketed bundle in his arms, Aretha replied. 'It's at the lower end of the street, but Doc Walpole is here at dinner. I'll fetch him.'

She was back in seconds with the old doctor hurrying behind her. Coming up to Katz, easing the blanket back a little and gazing over his spectacles at the girl's face, he worriedly inquired. 'Does she have a fever?'

Whispering so that even Aretha wouldn't hear, Katz reported, 'I fear that it is cholera.'

'Have you experienced that disease previously?' Walpole asked, trying to sound calm but not succeeding. Katz nodded.

'Then let us take her down to my place without delay.'

'I'll come with you,' an agitated Aretha was moving away to fetch her coat, but Katz stopped her.

'Please stay here, Aretha. The child's homesteader parents are coming into town. They are riding in a buckboard, and it would help if you meet them and tell them where we have taken their daughter.'

'I'll be at the door when they arrive,' Aretha promised.

'All three of them dead!' an incredulous Clement Foy gasped when he opened the ranch house door to Sil Sontanna.

'I'm afraid so, Clem.'

'Then this is murder. All three of them were unarmed, and Katz must have pulled his gun on them.'

Shifting uncomfortably, using his left hand to support his right arm that was in a sling, Sontanna reticently explained. 'That wasn't how it was, Clem. Hay's skull was shattered by a kick from a horse, McCabe's throat was crushed and he choked to death, while Hillier's neck was broken.'

'This was all Katz's doing?'

'Him and the horse,' Sontanna replied with a wry smile that he wiped swiftly from his face on realizing that Foy wasn't amused. 'I reckon as how Katz did for McCabe and Hillier.'

'But all three of them were unbeatable saloon brawlers.'

'Which don't make things look to good for us, Clem.'

Reaching behind him to close the door leading into the sitting room to prevent his wife and his son from overhearing the conversation, Foy's brow creased into a worried frown as he sought clarification. 'What precisely do you mean by that, Sontanna?'

'Well, it was three against one,' the range boss said with a shrug, unable to resist adding. 'That is until the horse joined in.'

'There is nothing amusing about this,' Foy nastily pointed out. 'With Cusick's election causing uproar in town we are three men down, and Katz is obviously a menace. Added to that, is the fact that if it gets known that I sent three men to rough up Katz, that will have Sutton on the prod and he will run a lurid story in that dratted newspaper of his that will have everyone against us. There isn't a chance of any witnesses?'

'To say no could mean that I would be telling a lie. There are wheel tracks that I'd say were made through the gorge at around the same time the ground was all mussed up by the fighting that went on between our boys and Katz.'

'So somebody could have seen what happened?'

'It looks that way, Clem.'

Clement Foy was far from pleased at hearing this.

On reaching the room in Walpole's house that he kept separate as a surgery Katz still held Estelle Edwards in his arms while the fussy old physician made a mattress from folded blankets and laid it on a table. Tenderly laying the girl on the table, inexplicably experiencing a feeling of sadness at parting from her, Katz opened the blanket she had been wrapped in so that the doctor could begin his work.

Seemingly noticing Katz's damaged face for the first time, the elderly doctor said. 'You need to have that seen to.'

'Don't worry, Doc, I've seen to it.'

Coming close to squint at the blue/black swelling, Walpole remarked. 'I see no sign of that.'

'You weren't there,' Katz pointed out.

'I think we are talking at cross purposes, young man. Am I to gather from what you say that there is a dead man lying somewhere out there in the night?'

'There are three of them, Doc, all past human aid. But this

child needs your attention right away.'

With a nod of agreement, Walpole concentrated on examining the girl, in doing so he lost all of his habitual bumbling movements, impressing Katz with his professionalism. Then he took one step back and stood studying the patient in his usual, over-the-top-of-his-spectacles style. Moving closer he bent to gently lift one of the girl's eyelids to intently peer into the eye for a considerable time.

Stepping back to his original position, he said solemnly. 'Your diagnosis was absolutely correct, mister. . . ?'

'Katz, Jorje Katz.'

'Ah, yes, Jorje, Aretha mentioned you to me,' the doctor remembered with a little smile of amusement. 'It grieves me to have to say that I agree with you. This is cholera. I would much rather have been able to prove that you were mistaken.'

'I was hoping that I was wrong,' Katz admitted.

'It is bad news. What chance of survival does this poor little creature have? Do you happen to know her age?'

'Sorry, I know nothing about her. My guess when I first saw her was six or seven.'

With a slow uncertain shaking of his head, Walpole pondered. 'I am not sure. There is something about her that has me suspect that she is small for her age.'

'Is her age important?'

'Very important. You did well in getting her to me quickly. She is at an early stage of the disease with premonitory diarrhoea present. If I can effectually deal with that then dehydration will not follow and the full development of the disease will be prevented. But I can only administer the required treatment if a patient is over the age of eight years. We need to establish her age without further delay. You are probably aware that patients can die within a few short hours of the onset of cholera.'

'Her parents should be here by now,' Katz said. 'My horse is outside so I will ride to meet them and learn her age.'

'So you must,' the old doctor concurred, desolately continuing. 'Please hurry or—'

The doctor was stopped in mid-sentence by a banging on the door.

'Sounds like they have arrived, Doc.'

'Then we must pray that the answer to our question is the one that we need,' Walpole said, giving Katz a friendly pat on the shoulder. 'Let them in, Jorje. They had best not see their daughter in her present condition, so take them in to the side room on the left of the passageway. Ask them what we need to know, but don't tell the reason for asking. Doting parents are, understandably, likely to lie about a child's age in order to have the treatment administered. The result would be to hasten the girl's death.'

The banging on the door continued until Katz reached it and let in a frantic Joel and Heather Edwards.

Reluctantly holding the door open for Sheriff Ike Rownton to step inside his house, a far from welcoming Cusick complained, 'I hope this isn't a social visit at this late hour, Ike.'

'I don't want to be here, Bart. But earlier today I overheard you telling someone that you had sent this Jorje Katz out to the Edwards' place on business.'

'That's right. Why, what's happened?'

'Maybe it's not important,' Rownton hedged his bets lest he should anger Cusick. 'But do the Edwards have a young son or daughter?'

'Yes – a daughter. What's this leading up to, Ike?'

'I thought you'd like to know that Katz came galloping into town a little while since carrying something wrapped in blankets. He went into the hotel and came out with Doc Walpole, and they went down to the doc's place. Then, just before I came here I saw Joel Edwards and his woman arrive in a buckboard. Aretha Ryland was waiting for them and directed them down to the doc's place. Putting two and two together I came to the conclusion that it was an Edwards' kid that Katz rode in with.'

'I don't doubt that you are right,' an annoyed Cusick decided. 'What is that man up to? I sent him out there to get my money, or something in lieu of my money, not to help that squatter with his family problems. That no-account Katz hasn't been in Singing River for five minutes, Ike, and he's already running things his way. I heard down in Santa Fe that he was a maverick. He will have to be taught a lesson.'

So nervous that he stammered a little, Rownton made his position clear. 'I can't go up against him, Bart.'

'It never occurred to me to ask you. I want to teach him a lesson, not provide him with an easy human target, Ike,' Cusick sarcastically retorted, quietly but angrily adding. 'There are other ways to settle his hash.'

Cusick had become so irate by this time so that he didn't notice Rownton walk out of the house, closing the door behind him.

FOUR

'Estelle will be nine next birthday.'

Heather Edwards replied to Katz's question just as the old doctor shuffled into the room.

Katz turned to Walpole, raising his eyebrows in a silent question. Getting the message but not relishing giving the response it called for, the doctor frowned as he put a question to the worried mother. 'How long ago was her birthday, Mrs Edwards?'

'June, June the twenty-third.'

'Less than three months,' the doctor mused. 'It doesn't help that she is tiny for her age.'

'What is the problem, Dr Walpole?' Joel Edwards inquired.

'The problem is that the effective treatment for this disease can only be given to patients past the age of eight years.'

'Which includes our daughter,' a hopeful Heather whispered to herself rather than the others present.

'I don't doubt your word, Mrs Edwards,' Walpole promised her. 'What causes me something of a dilemma in this case is that your daughter's physique is not as robust as that of most children of her age, and I fear that the treatment may prove to be too much for her.'

'What is the treatment, Doctor?'

'Full doses of laudanum together with acetate of lead and bismuth.'

Steeling herself for the reply, Heather asked. 'What would happen if the treatment is too strong?'

'Please don't force me to explain that in words, Mrs Edwards.'

'What if Estelle doesn't have the treatment, Doctor?'

The old man stayed silent but the effect that this question had on him was the unspoken but daunting answer that the parents had dreaded. Realizing this they delayed answering and avoided looking at each other, neither of them wanting to influence the other into making a decision that could possibly kill their only child.

Then, after a brief exchange of glances with her husband, Heather said, 'Then please give our daughter the medicine.'

Walpole released a sigh so long and loud that it filled the room. He seemed so relieved, and at the same time made anxious by the parents' consent, that Katz could tell that the kindly doctor was suffering from apprehension regarding the awesome task that lay immediately before him. When Joel Edwards spoke the doctor jerked, seemingly coming back from somewhere far distant at the sound of the father's voice.

'You have Heather's and my consent,' Joel said. 'But the way things are we are unable to afford to pay you even one cent, Doc.'

With a wan smile the old man gestured towards his surgery. 'That fact means nothing, my friend. If I can, with the help of God, make that sweet little girl in there well, that is all the payment I could ask for.'

'God bless you, Doctor,' Heather sobbed as she spoke. 'Please give our daughter the only chance of survival that she has. Can we stay here overnight?'

Without hesitation the doctor replied. 'I do not believe that would be wise, Mrs Edwards. That may strike your husband and yourself as a blatantly uncharitable response on my part. It is for your own good, believe me. This is going to be a long night, a night of doubt and anguish that it is best the patient's loved ones are separated from.'

'But, as you say, this will be a night of doubt, and we couldn't bear to be away from here wondering whether everything is going well for our child, or if the worst has happened,' the distressed mother said before turning to Katz. 'If it wasn't for you we would have lost our daughter back at the homestead. So you have our complete trust. What would you advise?'

Not welcoming having this dreadful decision forced upon him, Katz knew that he had to shoulder it. He said. 'The doctor is speaking from long experience, which none of us three have. Therefore, while appreciating how difficult it will be for both of you to separate yourselves from Estelle at such a time, I believe the alternative will be even more harrowing for you. I have to take my horse that is hitched outside to the stable. If you both walk with me I am sure that I can get you a room at the Stageline Hotel.'

'But how can we stay there when we'd have no way of knowing what is happening here?' the mother sobbed.

'When I have stabled my horse and have you settled in the hotel, I will return to assist Dr Walpole in any way that I can,' Katz announced. 'When there is something that you should know, I will come to the hotel to tell you.'

As the Edwards reluctantly prepared to leave, the doctor spoke confidentially to Katz. 'Thank you for saying that you will come back, Jorje. It is very good of you. I now consider you as a friend so please use our friendship by calling me by my name, Abel.'

*

'Yours is the only vacant room in the hotel, Jorje,' Aretha advised as he stood in the hotel reception with Joel and Heather Edwards.

'They can have it for the night. It's roomy enough for two,' Katz decided.

'That's not true,' Aretha corrected him. 'You must have offended Cusick in some way. He's moved you to a tiny room on the ground floor, next to the kitchen.'

Not surprised at hearing this, Katz asked. 'Can Joel and Heather fit in there, Aretha?'

'I'll make them comfortable,' she replied confidently. 'What about you, Jorje, where will you spend the night?'

'I'll be at Doc Walpole's place, helping him with the little girl.'

Moved by this, Aretha whispered. 'I knew from the first moment I met you that you are a good man, Jorje.'

'Believing that means that you'll be badly hurt when you learn the truth.'

'I'm sure that there is no truth I could learn that would change my opinion of you,' she told him. 'You get away now, Jorje, and I'll settle these two good people in your room.'

'You promise to come here and tell us what is happening to Estelle, even if it is what we don't want to hear?'

'You have my solemn promise,' Katz assured the distressed mother.

'There is someone on duty here behind the desk all night,' Aretha assured them.

Walking a few steps to catch up with Katz as he was leaving, she whispered, 'If you are going to continue working for Cusick, you ought to know that you now have to pay for that poky room as well as all meals and drinks.'

'Thank you for letting me know, Aretha,' a grim-faced Katz said, giving her arm a friendly squeeze before heading for the door.

Common sense flooded into Cusick's mind in a powerful tide that had his anger rapidly abate. Yanking his front door open, he stepped out to see Ike Rownton had not had time to get more than a few yards up the street. He called out and the sheriff turned and walked back to stand in front of him, waiting nervously for him to speak.

Apologizing had never come easily to Bartholomew Cusick, but he accepted that it was vital that he did so there and then. 'I am sorry about the way I spoke to you just now, Ike. This Katz has got me as mad as all get out. He's fuller of wind than a bull in green corn time, and it was wrong of me to take it out on you. Come on in and we'll have a talk.'

With Rownton already having entered the house, Cusick, needing time to consider how to put his proposition to him, took a long while to close the door. Added to his wealth, becoming mayor had made him the most powerful man in Singing River. Yet he had to somehow get Jorje Katz back under control if he was going to retain his authority, which was maintained by fear not compassion.

Pointing to a Victorian circular sofa for the sheriff to take a seat, Cusick left an empty seat between them when he sat. 'I'll tell you my difficulty, Ike. As you know, I sent Katz out to rough up that squatter Edwards if it proved to be necessary. What he did was to bring the Edwards and their sick off-spring into town for treatment by Doc Walpole. That is going to send out the wrong message about me, weakening my authority. There will be talk that Bartholomew Cusick has gone soft, has turned into some kind of skeery coot bent on helping out those he should be kicking into line.'

'We can't have that, Bart,' Rownton said simply because he felt that he should say something at that point.

His reckoning was that Cusick probably believed what he had just said. But the truth was that Katz had served his purpose on election day, and Cusick now regarded him as a menace. He now wanted to get rid of the gunfighter, and what that would involve unnerved Rownton. He shivered as he heard Cusick start talking again.

'I've got a plan. Now don't go getting all skeered-like, Ikey. Having you face Katz ain't going to gain me nothing but a dead sheriff. It'll be easy, Ike. All you need is that Winchester rifle you keep down at the jail, plus a little help from "Alley" Stevens. He'll set the target up for you.'

'Al Stevens is wholly unreliable, Bart,' Rownton protested. That was an inadequate description of the town drunk who had got the name Alley, Al for short, from spending every night in drunken slumber lying in some alley between buildings.

Taking a half-eagle gold coin from his pocket, Cusick placed it on a table saying, 'There's five dollars. Give that to Stevens and he'll be reliable long enough to do what you tell him to do.'

Two hours had passed since Katz had returned to the doctor's surgery. Ignorant of what was required of him he had relieved the old doctor of the heavy work. That didn't trouble him like the task of restraining the sick little girl while Doc Walpole had performed his ministration.

'The diarrhoea has ceased,' the old doctor neutrally announced in his muffled way of speaking.

'Is that good or bad, Abel?'

'If I knew the answer to that I would be a happy man. If we have caught it in time, then we have beaten the cholera. It will not develop.'

'What if we haven't caught it in time?'

'Let us leave that frightening prospect until, or if, it becomes necessary to face it, my friend. We should know in an hour or so. There is nothing we can do now but wait, so let us take a chair each and try to get some rest.'

Katz's chair, like the doctor's, was a comfortable one but sleep eluded him. An occasional slight noise from the young patient, though little more than a partly smothered whimper, constantly reminded him of the desperate plight of the child. His concern for her took priority over making plans for his own future. His liaison with Cusick, such as it had been, was now well and truly at an end for several reasons.

Though he hadn't been aware of it, he had eventually been overtaken by exhaustion. He realized this abruptly when he was awakened by Walpole shaking him by the shoulder and urgently calling his name.

'Jorje, Jorje, I need your help!'

As consciousness returned, Katz could detect what sounded like the low whining of an injured animal. Puzzled by this at first, he then came fully awake to realize the sound was coming from where Estelle Edwards lay in the centre of the room. The continuous sound signalled that the little girl was suffering intense agony, and was distressing to hear.

In a sorrowful whisper, the doctor informed him. 'I regret that we have to face the worst.'

On the first floor of the disused bakery, Sheriff Ike Rownton stood peering out through the partly open door through which old Ned Kent used to hoist up sacks of wheat from wagons. With a Winchester rifle in one hand and holding the now dysfunctional winching gear with the other, he carefully leaned out hoping to see Al Stevens. But he saw that the moonlit street was empty. An oil lamp glowed in one window of the doctor's house but all was quiet.

With the odds on Alley Stevens not letting him down discouraging, Rownton had started to fret. Cusick had made it sound easy when he had explained the plan to him. In this high position he just had to wait until Stevens caused a commotion that would bring Katz out of the surgery. With Stevens having hightailed out of harm's way, all he had to do was take Katz out with one shot. But as the time dragged on without Alley making an appearance, so the sheriff became increasingly nervous about what lay ahead of him.

Then he didn't know whether it was relief or panic that swept through him as he saw Stevens making his way unsteadily down the street towards him. Though staggering a little the town's drunk was in better condition than Rownton had dared to hope he would be.

'Is there no hope, Abel?'

Shaking his head slowly and dolefully before replying to Katz's question, the old doctor said, 'The diarrhoea has ceased without any of the encouraging signs that I expected to see. It would seem that some kind of complication has set in.'

'What is the answer to that?'

'The only available remedy is to bleed the child.'

'Then that is what we must do.'

Shaking his head yet again, slower and more sorrowfully this time, Walpole clarified the situation. 'Draining the little one's blood is said to relieve tension on constricted arteries and permit poisons to drain from the body, but I have three reasons for hesitating to do so. The first is that I have no leeches to attach, which is the relatively painless method. The second is to lance the flesh, which will cause this child even more pain that she is suffering at the moment. Thirdly, there are now serious doubts, which I most certainly share, about the efficacy of this treatment.'

'The prospects sure aren't encouraging,' Katz morosely commented.

'A small dose of red pepper might have been useful if given at the same time as the opiates, but it is too late now, Jorje.'

As Walpole finished speaking the glass of the surgery window shattered with an explosive sound and a stone thudded on the floorboards between the feet of Katz and the doctor. Shaken by the incident, the doctor looked at Katz in bewilderment.

'Stay here, Abel,' Katz said, leaving the room.

Slowly opening the front door he cautiously looked out into the street. There was no one in the immediate vicinity. He stepped out, his hand on the butt of his holstered .45. From the corner of his eye he caught a movement to his right and quickly turned to see a figure running off. From experience he knew that in darkness it was easier to see close to the ground. Drawing his gun he dropped to one knee while taking careful aim at the fleeing man's legs.

As he squeezed the trigger and saw the running man lurch sideways and then fall to the ground, so did the crack of a rifle shot fill the silent night. Feeling the hot breath of a bullet brush past his neck, Katz instinctively dived to lie face down in the dirt.

With a corner of the doctor's premises just a few feet in front of where he lay offering the chance of concealment in darkness, he was aware that he would risk his life if he moved. But neither could he indefinitely stay where he was. Needing to know the position of the rifleman he made his mind up. Swiftly rising on to his hands and knees, he did a scrambling crawl around the corner as a second rifle bullet splintered the wooden wall of the building just inches above him.

Having seen the flash of the rifle come from the first storey of a building directly across the street, he quickly devised a strategy. Getting to his feet in what was a passageway between two buildings, he ran to the far end to emerge into a wide alleyway. Moving fast he was relieved to reach another gap between buildings, which he sped along to come out into the main street just some fifteen yards further down from the doctor's house.

Crossing the street he moved along in the shadow close to buildings until he reached where the man with the rifle was concealed in a building that he gathered was an unoccupied former bakery. Finding the front door ajar, he eased it open far enough to step inside. Standing completely still he heard a slight movement overhead.

It was no more than the scuff of a foot but it was confirmation that the man who had tried to kill him was still in the building. With difficulty in the darkness he could make out a wooden staircase against the wall opposite to him. Though it provided access to the floor above, to climb the staircase would make him an easy target.

Anxious about having left the old doc to cope alone, and worried about the sick girl, Katz was struggling to think up a viable strategy to deal with the man who had attempted to kill him, when a voice called from the floor above,

'Is that you down there, Katz?'

Not recognizing the voice, he called back with a question of his own. 'Who's asking?'

'This is Sheriff Ike Rownton.'

'It's me, Rownton, and I figure that you and me have got a score to settle.'

He heard Rownton walk over to stand close to the top of

the stairs, from where he said. 'We are both men of the world, Katz. There ain't no point in one of us dying because we have become involved in some no-account shecoonery that ain't no business of ours.'

'You made it your business a short while since by taking two shots at me across the street, Rownton.'

'That weren't nothing personal. I was obeying Bart Cusick's orders.'

'A sheriff is paid to uphold the law, not to take orders from anyone,' Katz replied in disgust.'

'That ain't how it works hereabouts,' Rownton protested. 'Cusick is the biggest toad in the puddle here in Singing River. I was a John Law to be reckoned with at one time. Them days have gone for good, I knows that, but I've sure had enough of having Cusick treat me like a coot, and I intend to ride out of this town tonight and never come back.'

'You are free to do so, once you have got past me,' Katz told him sardonically.

'There's no call for that kind of talk, Katz. You can't come up here to get me, as I'll put a bullet in your head as soon as it shows at the top of the stairs.'

'That sure is right. But you can't stay up there forever, and I'm a right patient man, Rownton.'

This had the sheriff remain silent for some time, then in a wheedling tone he voiced a proposition. 'The sensible thing to do is you let me come down and walk out of here. You have my word that I will ride straight out of town and never come back.' Considering this for some while, Katz could see the logic of it. But he detested the thought of letting Rownton, who had twice tried to kill him, walk away. But weighed against that was his need to get back to Walpole's place. The doc, Heather and Joel Edwards and, above all, the doc's tiny patient, were relying on him. Seeing it that way told him there was no decision to make.

'I agree,' he called up to Rownton. 'Throw down your rifle.'

'Do I have your word, Katz?'

'You have my word.'

The sheriff's Winchester .30-.30 came clattering down the stairs to slam loudly against the wooden floor. Not going forward to pick it up, which would make him an easy target for Rownton at the top of the stairs, Katz ordered. 'Now your hand gun.'

A revolver came fast through the air to smash against the rifle on the floor. About to move forward to pick up the weapons, Katz's normal caution that had been temporarily driven out by concern over Estelle Edwards, returned. Was he missing something? Thinking hard brought up the memory of when he had first seen Rownton. It had been in Cusick's office, Katz realized, and this sharpened his recall and he saw an image of Rownton wearing two crossed gunbelts.

'Now your second handgun, Rownton,' he shouted.

This weapon swiftly followed the first to come down colliding with the other guns that lay on the floor. Walking over to the foot of the stairs, Katz first picked up the rifle and threw it over to the corner of the room. Then he did the same to one of the two revolvers, and was reaching for the second handgun when his reliable sixth sense kicked in to alert him to danger. Still bending over ready to pick up the remaining weapon, he turned his head slightly and from the corner of his eye saw the silhouette of Ike Rownton standing at the top of the stairs.

The right hand of the sheriff's silhouette was holding a gun. The gun was pointing down at Katz.

*

Heather and Joel Edwards' worry over their daughter made it impossible for them to relax, and sleep was out of the question. Aretha shared their concern, and the three of them had spent hours in her private rooms with her, drinking cup after cup of coffee.

'I thought he would have been here by now,' Joel said, referring to Katz.

'If Jorje promised to come to tell you the moment there is something to report, then you can rely on him to do so,' Aretha assured him in defence of her new-found idol.

'My mother was always saying that no news is good news,' distraught Heather reminisced. 'I pray to God that she was right. It is good of you to take us in, Miss Ryland. We couldn't have gone all the way back home worrying about what was happening to Estelle.'

'We'll be lucky if we have a home to go back to,' Joel unhappily remarked. 'Cusick is a ruthless man who is capable of anything.'

A worried expression on her face, Heather came in quickly. 'I hope Mr Cusick isn't a friend of yours, Miss Ryland?'

'I'm Aretha, Heather,' Aretha responded with a kind smile. 'No, Bart Cusick is no friend of mine, far from it. But he does own this hotel.'

'Then he'll be sure to punish you for having us in here,' Joel exclaimed worriedly.

'Don't worry, Joel,' Aretha consoled him. 'Cusick knows better than to try anything like that on me.'

Cursing himself for being caught out, Katz was aware that he had to act fast if he was to survive. Straightening up and going for his gun as he swung round to face the stairs, he pulled the trigger. But the report of his shot and that of

Rownton's were simultaneous. His right leg was knocked out from under him and he fell heavily to the floor.

Lying on his back with his right leg useless and trying to push with his left leg in an effort to roll on to his stomach and get into a kneeling position, he heard Rownton tumbling down the stairs. Partly succeeding in his attempt to roll over, Katz was knocked flat on to his back as the sheriff's heavy body landed on top of him. Pinned down, he first heard Rownton's laboured breath that was then followed by the unmistakable sound of the death rattle in the sheriff's throat.

It took all of Katz's depleted strength to push the dead body off him. Lying still to recuperate, he felt the pain begin in his thigh and was conscious of blood running down his leg. In an effort that caused him agony and exhausted him, he somehow managed to get to his feet.

Dragging his injured leg behind him, he made it out of the building and across the street to the doctor's house. Going in, he stopped in the passageway to recover enough strength to make it to the surgery. As he moved slowly on, the eerie stillness inside the house convinced him that he should expect the worst.

FIVE

Having earlier heard two rifle shots from further along the street, Cusick had relaxed, certain that Ike Rownton had just rid the town of the troublesome Jorje Katz. But now he heard the sound of more muffled shots, so that he deduced, incredible though it seemed to him in the circumstances, the two rifle shots from Rownton had been ineffective and Katz had gone into the building after him. Cusick was under no illusion what the outcome of that would be. The sheriff was not in Katz's class as a gunfighter.

That presented him with a dilemma. The chances were that only one of the two men in the bakery building would come out alive, and that would not be Sheriff Ike Rownton. Though Rownton's ability as a gunfighter had recently diminished, he was still the only enforcer that Cusick had. He realized now that he had made a mistake in alienating Katz.

Tempted to walk up the road to determine what had taken place at the bakery, he surrendered to his innate cowardice and went back into his house, closing the door. A worried man, he was aware that he had to swiftly get rid of Katz, who wasn't the kind of man who could be driven out of Singing River.

Recognizing that Katz had to be gunned down, a new plan

was already beginning to form in his mind as he made his way up the stairs to bed.

Opening the door to the surgery to see the doctor sitting in his chair, awake but with his open eyes plainly unseeing, increased Katz's worry. Worry that transmuted into despair as he saw how still was the small body of the child patient lying on the operating table in the centre of the room. Hampered by his injured leg he made his way across to put a hand on the old doc's shoulder and gently shake him.

This had no affect. The doc's sightless eyes stared past him. Desperate now, Katz grasped the old man's shoulder and shook him harder. Jerking violently, his legs kicking out, the doc became fully conscious but was plainly disorientated. First looking at Katz without knowing who he was, recognition slowly dawned on him.

'Jorje, you are back.'

'The girl, Abel?' Katz inquired urgently. 'Is it my fault for not being here to help?'

'I don't understand?'

'She is lifeless, not breathing.'

Leaping out of his chair the old man ran across the room to the girl. Hurriedly putting on his spectacles he peered closely at his patient, laying his hands on her before turning to Katz.

'She is breathing regularly.'

'I am sorry. I thought . . .' Katz murmured as the sympathetic doctor came to him and put an arm round his shoulders. 'She looked so still when I came into the room. It seemed that she had died and you were in shock.'

'She has tiny lungs, Jorje, and I am an old man who, exhausted but happy, collapsed in his chair.'

'You are saying that she is out of danger?'

Nodding and smiling, Walpole replied confidently, 'She passed through the crisis soon after you left, Jorje, and is now completely clear of cholera. All the child requires now is rest and wisely dispensed nutrition. Now, you have been wounded in the leg. Tell me what happened?'

'The *hombre* who smashed your window is lying out there in the street somewhere.'

'Let him lie there,' the old doc said with a callousness that was out of character.

'The window breaking was a ploy to get me outside, Abel,' Katz explained. 'I was drygulched from that old bakery across the street. It was the sheriff with a rifle.'

'Rownton? Then Bart Cusick is out to get you.'

'He failed this time. His sheriff buddy is lying dead across the street.'

'Good gracious!' the doctor exclaimed. 'Let me see to that leg of yours now. By the look of the way the blood has formed on your trouser leg I am certain that the bullet is still in your thigh.'

'Leave it for now, Abel. The girl's parents are waiting to hear from us. I'll be back as soon as I put their minds at rest.'

Aretha and the Edwards sprang to their feet when Katz entered the hotel. Both Heather and Joel found it impossible to ask the question they frantically wanted an answer to, and it was Aretha who spoke for them. 'How is she, Jorje?'

'She is out of danger,' Katz replied, pausing as Aretha and Joel sighed loudly in relief while Heather wept. 'Doc Walpole will be keeping her at his place until she is fit to return home.'

'Thank you. Thank you so much,' Heather managed to express her gratitude.

'We owe you everything,' Joel said, now close to tears himself.

'You owe me nothing,' Katz assured him. 'I can see that none of the three of you have had any sleep. You can catch up with some rest now.'

Shaking his head, Joel explained, 'Heather and me have to head for home. The animals need feeding and there's other chores to be taken care of.'

'Get some rest until sunup and I'll ride out with you,' Katz offered.

'Do you believe that is necessary?' Heather gasped.

'Probably not, but I'd feel easier if you would agree.'

'You have done so much for us,' Joel protested before self-consciously adding, 'But I admit that I'm scared about what Cusick might do now.'

'Then I'll call for you here at sunup,' Katz stated.

He was leaving when Aretha stayed him by placing a hand on his arm, concern on her face as she remarked, 'The leg of your trousers is soaked with blood, Jorje. Are you badly hurt?'

'It isn't anything serious. I'm going back to the doc's right now to get it fixed, Aretha,' he replied. 'Don't worry about me. You get yourself some sleep.'

With the permission of Preacher Isaac Donne, who sat beside him at a table facing a gathering of seated townsfolk, Meredith Harland had called an early-morning meeting in the church hall when he had learned of the death of Sheriff Ike Rownton.

'I thank you all for coming here, losing time at the start of what I am sure is a busy day for you all,' Harland addressed the crowd. 'Probably most or all of you have heard of the death of Sheriff Rownton.'

'Good news travels fast,' someone caused laughter by shouting from the rear of the hall.

Newspaperman Jeremiah Sutton stood to say, 'I know this

isn't a joking matter, Meredith, otherwise you wouldn't have brought us here. Nevertheless, Ike Rownton was a Cusick man, a sheriff in name only. I doubt that you'll find one mourner among all the folk gathered here.'

'I'm not looking for mourners. Doc Walpole informs me that Rownton was killed while attempting to bushwhack Jorje Katz, a visitor to our town.'

A tall man stood up in the second row from the front. 'I hear tell it was this Katz guy what killed the sheriff.'

'That is correct,' Harland replied.

'And is it correct that Al Stevens was found lying in the street this morning having bled to death after being shot by Katz?'

'Yes,' Harland confirmed. 'Stevens threw a stone through Doc Walpole's window when the doc was struggling to save the life of a child. He was also involved in a failed attempt to kill Jorje Katz.'

'We seem to be barkin' at a knot here, if you don't mind me saying so, Meredith,' Zak Horton spoke up. 'I can't waste time as folk get right grumpy if I don't open up my store on time. Could you tell us what we are here for?'

'I sure can,' Harland replied, pleased to elucidate. 'Ike Rownton was over the hill, we are all aware of that. Even so, he was Bart Cusick's right-hand man here in Singing River. There was no man locally who could risk going up against him. Now he's gone, which leaves Cusick out on a limb. Desperate men resort to desperate measures, so it is essential that we must act sooner rather than later to protect our town against Cusick. I recommend that here and now you good folk elect yourselves an alternative council to the one that has Bart Cusick as mayor.'

'I agree,' Jermiah Sutton said firmly. 'And I propose that we make Meredith Harland our new mayor.'

'I second that,' Jem Fraser, the town's handyman, solemnly declared.

Sutton called for a show of hands and the vote was unanimous. He said. 'Right, Mayor Harland, pick your council.'

'I suggest that we begin with a council of six,' Harland proposed. 'So I ask those of you who are willing to stand for council to present yourselves for election.'

'I would first like to nominate Preacher Isaac Donne,' Jeremiah Sutton stated.

Standing to a tumult of applause, Preacher Donne, a gentle, highly respected man approaching middle-age, expressed his willingness to serve while setting out his misgivings. 'I accept that something has to be done swiftly, as Meredith says. The plan he has put forward is not only sound, but it is impossible to come up with any other option. But I am conscious that in setting up in opposition we are likely to be creating a situation that will lead to war.'

'As Isaac rightly says, we have no other choice,' Zac Horton declared. 'I second Jeremiah's proposal for Preacher Donne.'

This proposal was immediately seconded and voted on. Then four more men, Sutton, Horton, Frazer, and Ebenezer Forest, who ran the Wells Fargo office in town, were voted in as councillors in quick succession. Satisfied with the outcome of the meeting called by Harland, the townsfolk were preparing to leave the hall when Preacher Donne made an observation.

'There is one more important item I must raise, Meredith. That is to remind you that we are now without a sheriff.'

'I have not overlooked that fact, Isaac,' Harland rejoined. 'We couldn't find a man more suited for the position of sheriff than Jorje Katz. I intend to offer him the appointment.'

The tall man, who had earlier questioned the deaths of Rownton and Stevens during the previous night, got quickly to his feet to challenge Harland. 'I guess that I am mistaken. Are you telling us that the sheriff you intend to appoint is the man who shot dead our sheriff?'

'If you knew the circumstances under which Rownton was shot you would not have asked that question,' Harland retorted. 'I will proceed with my intention to offer Katz the position. If he accepts, then you have a democratic right to challenge that appointment. This meeting is now closed.'

Heather and Joel Edwards stood at the door of their home watching Jorje Katz ride away. They had been relieved to come back to find everything in order, yet the immediate future worried both of them. Though missing their daughter, the very real possibility that Cusick would soon resume his campaign to drive them from their land, made them thankful that Estelle was on the mend and safely away from the danger that they would shortly be facing.

Joel was aware that Cusick's motive was not the money they owed him but the fact that they had water on their homestead. That was a precious commodity to ranchers like Clement Foy whose business was rapidly expanding. Cusick could get a high price for the Edwards' place if he foreclosed. With a judge on his payroll, Cusick would have no problem in making what on paper would be a legal foreclosure later backed up by gunsmoke.

'He's a good man,' Joel remarked to his wife, referring to Katz. 'And a hard man. It took the doc more than an hour to remove that bullet from his thigh, yet now he shows no sign of having been shot.'

'I know that, Joel. For the first time in months I felt really safe while he was here with us.'

'Try not to worry, Heather. As he told us, when back in town he can protect our child if necessary while on the lookout for any threat to us. He gave me his word that if anything like that should occur he will ride out here at once.'

As Joel took her hand and they walked into their cabin she couldn't shake off a sense of dark foreboding.

Katz was puzzled when entering the Goldliner Saloon on his return to Singing River. Ordering whiskey he sensed that he was the subject of the covert interest of just about everyone in the saloon, including the bartender who was serving him. He guessed that this had to be connected with his shooting of Sheriff Rownton but he couldn't understand why this should create such an atmosphere.

He was pondering on this when Carmencita walked over to him and said in her semi-humorous style, 'Buy me a drink and I'll tell you your fortune, mister.'

'I'm not staying long, Carmencita.'

'It won't take long. From what I've been hearing you don't have much of a future.'

'Maybe I should buy you a drink,' Katz relented, signalling to the bartender.

'Then I will begin,' Carmencita began mock-seriously. 'You will soon have a meeting with the mayor of Singing River that will dramatically change your life.'

'The next meeting I have with Cusick will change his life dramatically,' Katz told her grimly.'

Dropping her fortune-telling pretence, Carmencita said. 'A lot has happened while you were out of town today, Jorje. We now have two councils and two mayors; Mayor Harland and Mayor Cusick. It is Mayor Harland who wants to meet you. He wants to offer you the job of sheriff.'

Surprised by this, Katz delayed replying, but Carmencita

pressured him. 'Will you accept his offer, Jorje?'

'Perhaps I will, perhaps I won't,' was Katz's answer. 'I haven't eaten all day, so most important to me right now is finding some food.'

'I made sandwiches for myself earlier that I was about to eat when I saw you arrive. There are more than enough to share with you. They are in my room.'

'If you are sure,' Katz accepted her offer. 'Empty your glass and I'll get us both another drink to take with us.'

'You didn't come to our meeting this morning,' Meredith Harland mentioned to Aretha as she passed the table where Preacher Donne and he were eating dinner in the Stageline Saloon. When she paused, he looked around to check there was also a waitress serving tables, and then added. 'Have you got a few moments to spare?'

'The main rush is over,' Aretha replied, pulling out a spare chair to join them at the table. 'How can I help you?'

'We have no wish to offend you, Miss Ryland, so tell us if we have been misinformed,' Isaac Donne nervously said.

'Don't worry, Preacher Donne, I'll let you know if you cross the line. I'm often accused of being too straightforward.'

'I would say that is an admirable trait,' Harland assured her. 'I will come straight to the point. The subject we would like to discuss is Jorje Katz who, probably at least partly due to his lifestyle, is largely an unapproachable character. We understand from the doctor that since he came to Singing River you are the only one he has related to. Please understand that the request we are about to make to you is of vital importance to this town, otherwise we wouldn't dream of proposing something so personal.'

'I have always held Preacher Donne and you in high

esteem, Mr Harland, so go ahead and make your proposition. Should I find it necessary to refuse I will do so calmly and politely.'

'Thank you for being so understanding,' Isaac Donne smiled kindly at her.

Doing some deep thinking before speaking, Harland then said, 'You will have learned of Sheriff Rownton's death and that we found it essential to form an alternative local administration authority to that which has Bartholomew Cusick at its head. This will doubtless displease Cusick, whose response is likely to be catastrophic for this town and its inhabitants. Our newly formed council will put in place measures to protect the townsfolk and their interests. We have the power to make these regulations but lack the wherewithal to enforce them.'

'Which is where Jorje Catz comes in,' Aretha made a quiet voiced guess.

'Exactly,' Isaac Donne confirmed that she had it right. 'My calling prevents me from condoning killing or violence of any kind. Nevertheless, such is the situation here that I can envisage no other course of action. I am further persuaded by Jorje Katz's reputation that he is a man of principle and not a mindless killer.'

'Our fervent hope is that you may agree to broach to Katz the idea that he accepts an appointment as sheriff,' Harland tactfully explained.

'I am prepared to do that,' Aretha granted. 'Though I will not attempt to influence his decision in any way. Jorje is very much his own man, and the conclusion he reaches will be his and his alone.'

'I admire your ethical stance, Miss Ryland,' Isaac Donne praised her.

'Most certainly,' Harland concurred. 'We could not have

wished for a more moral response, and I express my gratitude for your assistance, Aretha.'

Clement Foy was saddling up in the corral of his Six Bar Six ranch. Straightening up after tightening the cinch, he looked in amazement at an approaching solitary rider. He blinked twice in disbelief at what he was seeing, but he had been right the first time. Bartholomew Cusick, his arch enemy, was on his land and heading towards him. Why? That was a simple one-word question to which Foy had no answer. Turning with his back to Cusick he fiddled with the saddle and reins; waiting.

'Good morning,' Cusick politely began, continuing when Foy neither turned to face him nor verbally responded. 'I appreciate why I am unwelcome here, Foy, but I come on a mission that is equally as important to you as it is to me.'

Swinging round to face him, fixing him with a glare of pure loathing, Foy said harshly, 'There is nothing in this world that would make me and you equal, Cusick. But as you rode out all this way I will give you two minutes to explain.'

Swinging one leg up on the pommel in front of him, Cusick began hurriedly. 'Things have changed suddenly and drastically in town. Meredith Harland has set up a council in opposition to the democratically established authority, with himself as the mayor.'

'Now that sure is interesting news,' Foy drawled. 'But it does not affect me in the slightest. However, I can see that it is one heck of a problem for you, Cusick.'

'I haven't yet given you the full story, Foy,' Cusick put in quickly. 'Sheriff Ike Rownton is dead, gunned down last night by Jorje Katz.'

Foy struggled not to let his amusement show as he commented. 'That's not much of a loss, as Ike Rownton was never much of a sheriff.'

'I can't argue with that, Foy, but the man Harland has selected to replace him will be raising Cain from the minute he pins on the silver star.'

An instant premonition hit Clement Foy hard. It raised prospects so worrying that as a religious man he experienced an uncommon urge to pray that the omen that had come so suddenly was wrong. Then Cusick dashed his hopes.

'Harland is going to offer the sheriff's job to Jorje Katz.'

The consequences should Katz agree to become sheriff, which Foy was certain he would, were fatal to his plan. Though he had wanted Meredith Harland as mayor, that was under the old regime, when it would have been easy to control him. With a new council and Katz as his enforcer, Harland was capable of running the territory with a firm hand.

'Why did you come to me, Cusick?'

'Because it is in your interest and mine to prevent a liaison between Harland and Jorje Katz.'

'Harland is not the problem,' Foy made clear. 'Without Katz, Harland would be no danger to us. Katz is our target. I am fortunate in having Sil Sontanna in my employ. He will be eager to call Katz out, and despite the reputation that Katz has as a gunfighter I do not see him, or anyone else for that matter, capable of beating Sontanna to the draw. I never believed that the day would come when I would consider you as an ally, Cusick. But I now suggest that you come up to the house and we'll discuss this matter fully.'

'I welcome the chance to do so, Clement,' Cusick grovelled. 'Immediate action is needed to prevent Harland's venture gaining strength.

Having enjoyed Carmencita's company, Katz had spent

longer than he had intended with her. Consequently the evening meal at the Stageline Hotel had passed its peak and many of the diners had left when he arrived.

'Your table in the corner is ready for you, Jorje,' Aretha informed him after they had exchanged greetings. 'Your dinner will be with you very soon. I haven't eaten, so I wondered if I might join you.'

'You will be very welcome,' he assured her.

When they were settled at the table and had begun eating, she mentioned the happenings of that day. 'Meredith Harland has set up a town council of his own.'

'A girl at the Goldliner told me that.'

'Carmencita?'

The way she asked the question had a dual effect on him. It felt good to have a beautiful, intelligent woman so intensely interested in him, yet contradictorily it somehow lessened him as a man. Self-sufficient throughout his life, needing to be with Aretha was both a strange and somehow disturbing experience.

'Yes,' he replied. 'She also suggested that Harland would want me to be the sheriff in place of Rownton.'

'That is true, Jorje. Meredith Harland ate here earlier with Preacher Donne. They asked me to find out how you would feel about becoming sheriff.'

'You know the Singing River people but I don't. What would you advise me to do, Aretha?'

'I agreed to tell you what they wanted, but refused to attempt to influence you in any way.'

'Nevertheless, I would welcome your opinion,' Katz appealed.

Frowning as she considered this, Aretha then said evenly. 'Very well, I will describe how I see the situation, but will make no comment on whether or not you should become sheriff.'

'That will be helpful.'

'I hope so. The situation is that Bart Cusick has spent a considerable amount of time and cunning establishing himself in a position of power in this town. Ambitious people are ruthless people, and Cusick is fanatically ambitious. In the last couple of days his triumph at becoming mayor has been ruined by the threat to his power. Harland and the other prominent people in town have everything to lose if they don't overthrow Cusick, while Cusick will be finished if they succeed. It will be a war of attrition, Jorje.'

Though accepting this, Katz reasoned, 'But all Cusick has is cunning; he has nothing with which to fight a war.'

'Don't be too sure of that,' she warned. 'This is nothing but my theory, and you probably won't wish to hear it.'

'I want to hear it, Aretha.'

'Well, here it is for what it's worth. Before the recent election for the mayor, Clement Foy supported Harland against Cusick as he believed that if Harland were elected he could control him. But now Harland has shown a strength no one guessed that he had. This has created a situation that, unlikely as it may seem, will lead to an alliance between Bartholomew Cusick and Clement Foy.'

'This means that Cusick will be able to rely on Sil Sontanna and the other renegades employed by Foy.'

'That's right. Harland and his buddies have recognized this will happen, which is why they want you on their side. Will you agree to be sheriff, Jorje?'

'I came to Singing River expecting to be a partner in a gold digging mission. That didn't happen, so I need some other way of earning money.'

Disheartened by this, Aretha warned. 'You will be in great danger from Sontanna and the rest of that Foy gang.'

*

Delighted by Katz having agreed to be appointed sheriff, Harland unlocked the jailhouse door in preparation for showing him around. 'There is a spacious room at the back that will be your living quarters. That will relieve you of the necessity of having a room in Cusick's hotel.'

'That's fine,' Katz acknowledged as they entered the building. 'Do I get a deputy?'

Bowing his head in embarrassment, Harland said apologetically. 'I am afraid not. Rownton had Charlie Daltrey as his deputy. Charlie is elderly and of little use other than as a jailer, so we paid him off as soon as we formed the new council. We have only one prisoner, and Zac Horton has been feeding him. Preacher Donne attempted to provide for his spiritual needs but he doesn't appear to have any.'

'I didn't know you had a prisoner,' Katz said, looking at the two empty iron cages in front of them.

'He's locked up a cell at the rear,' Harland explained. 'He is Fernando Hyer, who has committed no offence here in Singing River but is wanted for a stagecoach robbery and murder in New Mexico. Ebenezer Forest will know if Rownton has informed the appropriate authorities. If not, now that we can rely on you to send Hyer packing away from town, we might as well release him. He gave himself up to Ike Downtown without protest. But watch yourself, Jorje. I reckon as how he could lick his weight in wildcats.'

'Then I'd best start by taking a look at him,' Katz decided.

He followed Harland to a separate cage at the back of the building, in which a youngster in his early twenties, black-haired and good-looking, jumped up off his cot to sneer at Katz.

'Well lookee what we have here. A mail-order cowboy with a pretty star pinned to his chest. You are out West now, greenhorn, where men are men and you ain't going to last for long.'

'Maybe you are right, kid. But I'll enjoy what time I do have if I shut that big mouth of yours.'

'Talk like that's easy when there's iron bars keeping us apart.'

'Give me the key,' Katz ordered Harland.

'I don't think that's—' Harland gasped nervously.

Snatching the key to the cell from Harland, whose self-preservation instinct had him take several steps backwards, Katz unlocked the door of thick iron bars.

SIX

Seemingly to be bemused by Katz suddenly opening the door, Hyer was immobile for a few seconds. Then he lunged at Katz, throwing a vicious right hand punch at his head. With his open left hand Katz easily diverted Hyer's fist over his right shoulder before immediately driving his own right fist into a twisting punch to Hyer's stomach.

With the breath knocked out of him the prisoner jack-knifed forwards. Swiftly changing his fist to an open right hand, Katz drove it upwards to slam into Hyer's mouth and then rake up over his nose. Sent flying backwards on to his cot, the back of his head thudding against the bars, Hyer lay on the bed unconscious and bleeding heavily.

Harland panicked. 'Is he dead?'

'There's blood gushing from his mouth and nose,' a relaxed Katz observed. 'Dead men don't bleed, Harland.'

'But he could well die,' Harland nervously prophesized.

'If he does, then I will take full responsibility,' Katz volunteered. 'Lock him in and give me the key. I'll go up to the hotel to fetch my war bag and then come back to take a look at him.'

'We have a meeting of the council in the church hall at three o'clock this afternoon. We are going to thresh out a strategy for moving forward. It is essential that you are in attendance, Jorje.'

'I'll be there,' Katz promised.

'I thought that I would be seeing you regularly,' a disappointed Aretha reacted badly when Katz told her that he was moving to live in the jailhouse.

'Though I hate the idea of giving Cusick money, I will eat here every day, Aretha.'

'That's good to hear, Jorje,' Aretha said with a smile. 'To make sure that Bart Cusick is the loser I'll just charge you a quarter of the usual cost each time.'

'That will be theft, which means that as the sheriff I'll have to arrest you,' Katz grinned.

'I'll be happy with that providing we have the jailhouse to ourselves,' she cheekily told him. Then she became serious to ask, 'What happens with you now, Jorje? Have they said what they want of you?'

'They are having a meeting this afternoon and want me there, so I'll find out what's expected of me then. Harland and the others know that soon they will have a war to fight, and those who start and run wars, even the range wars I've been involved in, never venture where the bullets are flying.'

'So you'll be in the front line all alone.'

'That's what they will be paying me to do.'

'I know it will be impossible to dissuade you,' Aretha said despondently. 'So all I can do is pray for you.'

Greeting Katz with a sullen glare, Hyer was no longer bleeding but his top lip was bruised and his nose swollen. Unlocking the cell door and stepping inside, Katz left the door wide open.

'Am I about to get another beating?' the prisoner inquired.

'You wouldn't have got the first one had you not taken a swing at me,' Katz pointed out.

Thinking this over, Hyer lost much of his hostility as he admitted. 'I reckon as how that is true.'

'Then we are making progress,' Katz remarked. 'We'll get along fine if you keep your aggression in check and don't have so much lip.'

'The second bit's easy,' Hyer said tenderly touching his top lip. 'It hurts just to talk.'

'I can't say that I am not pleased to hear that. I have to leave you again right now, but I should be back in an hour or so,' Katz mentioned lightly as he went out of the cell.

Hyer called him back. 'You have left the door open, Sheriff.'

'It won't ever again be locked for you, Hyer,' Katz announced as he walked back to stand in the doorway.

'I don't understand.'

'Have you got a horse?'

'Yeah, the other guy wearing a star put it in some stables in town when he locked me up.'

'Good. I'm about to give you three choices, kid. You can ask me to lock the door and stay where you are while I contact the authorities in New Mexico to come and pick you up, or you can get your horse and ride out of town and stay away.'

Slowly shaking his head, Hyer said, 'If I stay I'll end up decorating a cottonwood, and I sure don't fancy being hanged. If I ride away from here I have nowhere to go. That's why I gave myself up so easily. What is the third choice you mentioned, Sheriff?'

'You stay and I take you on as my deputy.'

'Wow!' Hyer was shocked by this suggestion. 'Well I'll be danged. That idea appeals to me less than the other two did.

Finding myself on the right side of the law will call for a whole heap of adjusting. Can you give me time to think? It won't take me long.'

'Take all the time you need, kid. I'd say riding away as a free man sure as hell beats ending up wearing a California Collar,' Katz said as he walked away, leaving the cell door wide open.

Surprised at having been invited to remain at the Six Bar Six for lunch, a wined and dined Cusick felt good as a now friendly Clement Foy and Sil Sontanna walked him to his horse. Foy had explained that today was the day he paid his men and, as always, the whole rowdy bunch of them would be riding into Singing River for a night of drunken revelry.

'That will put Katz to the test, Bart,' Foy had explained. 'He comes with a reputation Billy the Kid would have traded his grandmother in for, but no one man could take on the wild Singing River multitude on pay night and survive. Jorje Katz will prove to be no exception.

'I'll make sure of that,' Sontanna had added.

Pleased at hearing this, Cusick had asked. 'Will you be there?'

'No, Sil won't,' Foy had answered for his straw boss. 'We don't want the trouble to look organized, like it would if Sil was there running things. Katz will be seen to have arranged his own demise. Whatever happens has to look natural.'

Now, as they had shaken hands with Cusick and stood watching him ride away, Foy asked Sontanna. 'How are you going to arrange it, Sil?'

'I'll use Danny McCauley and Rob Foster, our two best gunhands. They are real good. It's possible that either of them could get the drop on Katz but I want nothing left to chance. I'll get Danny to prod Katz into action, while Rob stays close by. They have to make sure that Katz is first in going for his gun. Then Rob can gun him down, with both him and Danny ready to swear that Danny had no intention of pulling his gun on a sheriff.'

'That's good thinking, Sil,' Foy chuckled, 'but with the sheriff dead there won't be any law in town to question what happened. Seriously though, Meredith Harland and Jeremy Sutton are sure to make a fuss and Preacher Donne will be sure to add his condemnation of the death of a sheriff. You are absolutely right in wanting to avoid turning the people against us. I'll leave it to you, Sil.'

'It will be done right, Clement,' Sontanna affirmed.

'Amen,' Foy reverently ended the conversation.

Pay day and the mayhem that Six Bar Six men and cowhands from surrounding ranches had previously caused in Singing River was the main subject discussed at the first meeting of the new town council. Jeremiah Sutton was keen to impress the danger points on Katz.

'The Goldliner Saloon is where the trouble will be centred,' the newspaper man explained. 'It is always crowded on these nights and when a problem occurs it is invariably of the kind that defies being sorted without someone innocent getting hurt or worse.'

'Not that Ike Rownton ever tried to sort out any lawlessness,' Zac Horton interjected.

Harland brought the meeting back to order by saying, 'Rownton is dead; Jorje Katz is the sheriff now.'

'That prompts a question I wish to ask Sheriff Katz,' Preacher Donne announced seriously. 'With the greatest respect, I need to know whether you intend to adopt a shoot first and ask questions afterwards policy?'

'Also with respect, Preacher Donne, someone pulling a

gun on you isn't likely to be interested in answering questions before pulling the trigger,' Katz answered.

Sutton continued where Katz had left off. 'We look to Sheriff Katz to enforce the law, not to determine what human defect makes people break the law, Reverend.'

'I am afraid we are digressing,' Meredith Harland interrupted. 'No doubt Isaac meant well but keeping the folk of this town safe is what we are asking of Jorje Katz. I know that we can rely on him to do that without resorting to any of the brutality and callousness we have experienced in the past. It was a mite high-handed of me to appoint Jorje as sheriff without first putting the appointment before the full council. So I will right that wrong by asking for a show of hands. All those in favour?'

Everyone present, including Preacher Isaac Donne, instantly raised their hands.

Fernando Hyer was still in his cell when Katz returned to the jailhouse. Standing to greet him, Hyer said. 'I'm still thinking on your offer, Sheriff. You could do me a favour that would help me reach a decision'

'You aren't exactly in a position to ask for favours, kid. But try me.'

'The John Law what brought me in here took my gunbelt with its holstered Colt peacemaker from me. I want it back.'

'Why?'

'Because I've narrowed the three choices down to one, and that isn't either staying here to be dragged back to New Mexico or remaining here as your deputy.'

'Seems to me, kid, that wanting your gunbelt means you're scared I was fooling you when I said you were free to ride out of town.'

'That did occur to me,' Hyer laconically replied.

'That answer has me suspect that you could be hoping to draw faster than me.'

'There ain't no chance of that,' Hyer firmly stated. 'That old-timer who brings me my grub told me who you are. I know better than to pull a gun on Jorje Katz.'

'How do I know you won't change your mind if I give you your gun?'

'You don't,' Hyer said with an almost shy smile. 'But I guess it wouldn't faze Jorje Katz if I did.'

'I've always known that there has to be someone faster than me, and maybe you are that someone, kid.'

'There's no chance of that.'

Going out of the cell, Katz beckoned for Hyer to follow him. 'Then you can have your gun. I've a busy night ahead so I'll trust you to make your way out of town. I'll settle the bill at the stables and tell Al Petain that you'll be coming to get your horse.'

'That's mighty nice of you, Jorje.'

Finding the gunbelt in a cupboard Katz passed it to Hyer. Buckling the belt on, Hyer gyrated his hips a little to settle it comfortably against him, and tied the holster to his right thigh before telling Katz. 'That feels real good.'

'I know the feeling,' Katz admitted. 'I have to go now. Don't let me down, Fernando.'

Startled by Katz's use of his first name, Hyer asked, 'What happened to calling me kid?'

With a faint smile on his face, Katz replied, 'The way you look since you strapped that peacemaker on it would be an insult. Remember what I said; don't let me down.'

'You have been straight with me so that won't happen, Jorje,' Hyer said, shaking hands with Katz.

The tense atmosphere of expectancy that had been building

up in the town since mid-afternoon, subdued the usual volume of conversation in the Stageline Hotel that evening. The disruption caused on previous pay nights was a memory that returned to haunt the good folk of Singing River on the approach of every new night of uncontrolled revelry. Sharing a table with Katz and Dr Walpole, Aretha Ryland's anxiety was evident in the question that she posed.

'What are the next few hours going to mean to each of us?'

'For me it means that I will have a busy night tending head injuries and broken limbs,' Dr Walpole complained.

Katz guessed that the astute and compassionate old doctor had deliberately kept his reply grumpily personal so as not to add to Aretha's worry. He avoided answering by asking an unconnected question. 'How is Estelle, your girl patient progressing, Abel?'

'She is doing really well. I anticipate allowing her to return home in the next day or so.'

'I'm pleased to hear that,' Aretha said with a sigh of relief. 'What about you, Jorje?'

'It couldn't be better news.'

'That wasn't what I meant. I know how upset you were over that little girl. I want to know what the next few hours will mean to you?'

'Whatever it is I'll just have to handle it.'

'That's not a proper answer,' Aretha protested.

'It's the only answer a man in Jorje's position can give,' the old doc said to help Katz, adding, 'You must think about yourself, Aretha.'

'You know that I lock up the hotel straight after the evening meal on pay day, Abel.'

'I do, but tonight is likely to be much worse than anything this town has experienced to date.'

'But if it is right that Cusick is now with Clement Foy, he is unlikely to allow Six Bar Six men to damage his hotel.'

'Having Cusick with him is just convenient for Foy,' Katz explained. 'Cusick will certainly be used for Foy's ends, but he definitely won't get any help from Foy in return.'

'Clement Foy is a religious man, so wouldn't it help if Preacher Donne were to have a word with him?' Aretha suggested.

This amused Doc Walpole. 'I fear that Foy's religious beliefs would drastically differ from those of Isaac Donne. Foy lives by the gospel of the gun providing that it is not he but one of his mindless and lawless disciples who is pulling the trigger.'

'Bart Cusick had plans for Singing River that have perturbed me for a long time,' Aretha declared. 'Now this dual council arrangement will mean that the slowly nearing disruption Cusick was going to cause the town is now a fast approaching catastrophe. Is there no one we can trust to avert this tragedy?'

'One step at a time, is my advice,' Doc Walpole responded. 'I can assure you that from sundown onwards tonight you can have total faith in Jorje Katz.'

Early evening saw the cowhands from outlying ranches begin riding into town. At first they arrived in small groups who quietly dismounted and hitched their horses outside the Goldliner Saloon before peacefully entering the place. This didn't ease the dread of townsfolk who knew they were witnessing the calm before the storm. Storekeepers fitted boards to their windows as shutters, while parents made hasty searches for children playing in the street and hurriedly took them to safety in their homes.

Less than an hour later the trickle of peaceable riders was

replaced by rowdyism as the whooping and hollering Six Bar Six employees arrived. The streets quickly emptied and Singing River became a ghost town with the exception of the Goldliner Saloon area.

Then Meredith Harland and the other five councillors came anxiously walking up the street, halting to stand opposite to the saloon with Preacher Donne's church at their backs. Unnoticed, they watched with disapproving interest the uninhibited antics of the young men across the street from them.

As more riders poured into town, they noticed that six of the revellers were observing them from across the street. At first there were jokes that the councillors couldn't hear, but which had the rowdies roaring with laughter. Then a youngster with shoulder-length yellow hair looked up at the small bell tower. Drawing his six-shooter, he called to attract the attention of those around him before holding the gun in both hands to take a steady aim at the church bell.

A mighty cheer went up as the bell loudly rang, drowning out a shout of protest from Preacher Donne who started to run across the street at the yellow-haired rowdy, mindless of the fact that he still held his smoking gun in his hand. Harland and the other councillors shouted at the preacher to come back, just as a newcomer rode into town and quickly took in the situation. Grinning as he watched Preacher Donne running, the rider reached to free his lariat from his saddle. Swinging it above his head and encouraged by the onlookers' cheers, he rode at Donne to neatly lasso him.

Yanking the rope to pin the preacher's arms to his sides, the horseman then dug in the spurs to ride off down the street. Pulled off his feet, Donne was dragged through the dust at speed. Some distance down the street the rider swung round to gallop back up and stop in front of the crowd outside of the saloon. Laughing as he dismounted, he ran to the preacher and wrapped the rope tightly around his legs.

Ignoring the remonstrations of Harland and the others, he straightened up and shouted a question at the crowd: 'Shall I brand him?'

There was a roar of laughter at this. Satisfied at having been the centre of attention, the rider rolled Preacher Donne this way and that to retrieve his lariat. Then as the councillors knelt beside their friend, he rolled the rope and replaced it on his saddle, hitched his horse and went towards the door of the saloon with the others.

Last in line, the yellow-haired man and the rider who had carried out the roping turned before entering the saloon. Exchanging grins as they saw the councillors bending over their prostrate friend the pair did a fast draw and fired several shots. Unaware that they weren't the targets, as the gunmen had fired high for effect and not to cause death or injury, the councillors ran off down the street, crouching low.

About to leave the hotel after finishing his meal, Katz was strapping on his gunbelt when he heard the old doctor's half whispered exclamation: 'Good lord, it has started early!'

Katz looked up to see that a dishevelled, breathless Meredith Harland had entered the hotel calling, 'Come quickly, Doc. They have attacked Isaac Donne. I fear that he is badly hurt.'

'I'll be right with you Meredith,' the old doctor said as he hurriedly put on his coat.

'Not without me you won't, Abel,' Katz said staying the elderly man by gripping his arm. Turning to Harland, he asked, 'What happened?'

Harland told the story of how the preacher had been distressed by one of the cowboys shooting at the bell, continuing in a shaky voice to described the roping of Donne and the enjoyment it had given the bunch of ruffians.

'And this is before they have had liquor,' a shocked Doc Walpole said quietly to himself.

'Where is the preacher now?' Katz asked.

'Lying in the street. We came under fire and had to leave in a hurry.'

When Harland, the doc and Katz left the hotel they found four agitated councillors waiting for them. Sighting Katz, Zac Horton cried out, 'We were forced to leave Isaac, Sheriff. The man who fired his gun at the bell took shots at us to drive us away.'

'Can you give me a description of the two men responsible?' Katz asked Harland.

'I can do better than that, Sheriff, I am prepared to come into the saloon with you and identify both of them.'

With a negative shake of his head, Katz said. 'No you won't. I can't do what I have to do while at the same time making certain that you are safe. It will assist me greatly if you describe these men.'

'That is easy to do where the one with the gun is concerned,' Harland replied. 'He is Rob Foster, young with collar-length yellow hair. The one with the lariat is more difficult, he—'

'Is Danny McCauley,' Jeremiah Sutton interrupted. 'Some time back I ran a story on that varmint. I can't remember the details, but I know that he is trouble.'

'Anything distinguishing about his appearance?' Katz inquired.

'McCauley is a rough-houser as well as a gunslinger, handy with his fists and his boots,' Sutton answered. 'You'll know him when you see him; a broken nose and shoulders as wide as a barn door.'

'That's good enough for me to find both of them,' Katz confirmed. 'I'm going to walk up to the Goldliner now. All of you follow me as you will be needed to carry Preacher Donne down to the doc's, but keep well back. If when I get there it is safe for you to join me, I'll wave a hand for you to come up.'

'I'll go first to examine Isaac,' Doc Walpole told the others, all of whom nodded agreement.

When Katz arrived outside the saloon the street was deserted apart from Preacher Donne lying motionless in the centre. A man standing in the doorway of the Goldliner turned away quickly to go back into the saloon, but not before Katz had caught sight of his long yellow hair.

As the five councillors moved in, the kneeling doctor looked up to report, 'My preliminary examination reveals bruising and numerous abrasions. Nothing more serious.'

'But he is unconscious,' Jem Fraser declared anxiously.

'A condition that I consider is due to shock,' the old doc said.

'That ain't surprising, seeing as how he's been dragged up and down the street,' Ebenezer Forest reasoned.

'Is it anything to worry about, Doc?' Sutton inquired.

'I am most concerned about it, Jeremiah.'

'Could it lead to his heart giving out?'

'It could cause many serious complications,' Doc Walpole answered. 'We must get him down to my place. The sooner I can bring Isaac round, the sooner I can judge how badly he has been affected by the abominable treatment he has been subjected to.'

'Right, gentlemen,' Jeremiah Sutton addressed his fellow councillors. 'Let us lift Preacher Donne up from the street and carry him to Doc Walpole's.'

'Lift gently,' the old doc ordered as he moved in to supervise. 'Two of you take his legs, and two his upper torso. Link hands under his back so that he is firmly supported.'

The councillors did as they were told, although they strained to get the moderately heavy body of the preacher up from the ground. Having achieved the lift they started off down the street, lumbering and staggering due to their awkward burden.

Going into the saloon, Katz took one sideways step to ensure there could be nothing but a wall behind him, then stood to study the predominately male assembly. He noticed Carmencita halt as she came down a stairway to his right, gripping the rail with both hands as she gazed worriedly at him.

To his surprise he saw Fernando Hyer leaning with his back against the bar and a glass in his hand. This meant one of two things to Katz: Hyer had either decided to have a drink before leaving town or, more likely, he was going to stay in Singing River. If that was the case, then Katz had no doubt that he could expect trouble from the young gunslinger.

He forgot Hyer completely when he spotted a young guy with long yellow hair who had to be Rob Foster. He was sitting with others at a group of tables at which sat drinkers and gamblers. First, taking careful note of his immediate surroundings, Katz then made his way toward the table at which Foster sat.

Noticing him approaching, three men sitting at a table to his left exchanged a few words, smiled at each other before one of them tilted himself and his chair back to block the gangway between tables. Not slowing his steady pace, Katz kicked out with his right leg to send the chair flying and its occupant crashing to the floor.

As the cowboy hit the floor the impact knocked his six-shooter out of its holster. Face flushed with rage, the fallen man quickly reached for the weapon. He had it in his grasp when Katz stamped on his wrist, walking on as the sound of bones cracking rose above the hub-hub of music and conversation.

Reaching Foster's table, Katz checked that he had the right man by asking. 'Is your name Rob Foster?'

'You must know it is or you wouldn't have asked,' Foster coolly answered.

'Then get up on your feet.'

Foster impressed his friends by briefly remaining seated before placing both hands on the table to push himself slowly upright. As this was happening Katz checked out the immediate area. There were quite a few watching the little scene, but they appeared to be no more than interested spectators. He could see no-one matching Sutton's description of Danny McCauley among them.

That left him no option but to be on the alert for when McCauley did appear, as Katz was confident that he would. McCauley wasn't his principal worry right then; this was Hyer, still stood at the bar to Katz's left and slightly behind him. Knowledge that this put him in danger from Hyer if the man now standing in front of him went for his gun, Katz made a slight movement so he could see Hyer from the corner of his eye.

'What do you want with me, Sheriff?' Foster arrogantly asked.

'I'll tell you when we get down to the jailhouse.'

'Why would I want to go down the jailhouse with you?'

'You don't have to want to go,' Katz firmly explained. 'You don't have a choice.'

'Then you're going to have to have a mighty good reason for taking me in.'

'I'm not going to argue with you. So let's get moving, Foster.'

'I don't think so,' a suddenly obstinate Foster announced with a shake of his head.

Accepting that trouble was about to follow, Katz noticed Danny McCauley appear at the front of the crowd. Though some distance away, the powerfully-built, flat-nosed man was close enough to be dangerous.

Taking a quick glance in Hyer's direction, Katz saw that he still leaned on the bar with a glass in his hand but Katz wasn't fooled by his apparent disinterest. This was a deliberate pose by the intelligent Hyer, who would be closely observing the scene.

Realizing that he had Foster, McCauley and Hyer to watch, Katz tensed for action as Foster's hand hovered over the handle of his holstered gun.

'I guess we ain't going to agree, Sheriff—' Foster started to say, but suddenly broke off and reached for his gun.

Katz drew fast, yet he had only just cleared the holster and Foster still hadn't drawn, when on the periphery of his vision, Katz saw that McCauley had a revolver aimed at him.

SEVEN

Getting hurriedly to her feet as Meredith Harland came into the hotel, Aretha asked, 'How is the Reverend Donne?'

'Badly shaken, but the doc says that no permanent damage as been done, Aretha.'

'Thank the Lord.'

'The pressing matter at the present moment is what is happening at the Goldliner Saloon,' an anxious Harland informed her.

'Have you heard anything, Mr Harland?'

'No. Coward that I am, I dread hearing what has occurred in that God-forsaken place. I find it distressful enough to know that Jorje Katz is all alone there facing the whole damn bunch of roughnecks that hold this town at ransom every month. I bitterly regret having put Katz in this position.'

'Is there any way you can help him?' Aretha inquired, close to pleading.

With a weary shake of his head, Harland made a shamefaced admission. 'There is no active part that we can play in this regrettable event. We are councillors, not gunslingers. We are guilty of appointing a new sheriff without anything like sufficient forethought. No matter how experienced and skilful he is, no one man can survive for long against the odds of Singing River's massive rowdy element. Sadly, it is too late to change anything now.'

Danny McCauley had the drop on him, Katz accepted that. It was entirely his fault. Unusually for him in such circumstances, he had mistakenly and fully concentrated on Foster. There was no time for self-recrimination. The situation was tense and had the unearthly silence that Katz had known many times before and recognized as the prelude to blazing guns and sudden death.

His disadvantage in the situation was clear to him, but if his time was up he was determined to take McCauley with him. He was also keenly aware of Hyer's position slightly behind him. If Hyer fired before McCauley, Katz knew that he would die without having an opportunity to take out McCauley, who was plainly enjoying playing up the edge he had on Katz by delaying pulling the trigger.

The way time slows at a crisis gave Katz a chance to think. How did he allow himself to get into this hopeless position? He hadn't lost his touch. Proof of that was the recent gunplay he had been involved in outside of the church hall at the election. Could it be that Aretha Ryland, taking up a permanent place in his mind, had affected his judgement? Never before had he felt this way about a woman. He had known many saloon girls yet couldn't remember a single one of them now.

Then his mind-searching ended abruptly as a shot was fired. McCauley hadn't pulled the trigger, and looked just as surprised as Katz was. It had to be Hyer, but how could that self-assured kid have missed him at such close range? Katz was in a dilemma: if he did a quarter turn to get Hyer, then McCauley would get him; to draw on McCauley first would only mean a reverse of that sequence. Either way he would be gunned, most probably without getting a shot off at either of the two.

Then Katz was stunned to see McCauley's surprised facial expression fade. His eyes went blank prior to him pitching forwards to slam face down on the floor and go through a series of what he recognized as terminal convulsions. Turning to face Hyer, prepared to take a chance by drawing, Katz saw that the kid was holding a smoking gun and smiling at him.

Hyer pointed at the gun that Katz was aiming at him and calmly advised, 'I guess you wouldn't want to shoot your new deputy after he'd just saved your life, Sheriff.'

Everything that had just happened in a split second ran clearly through Katz's mind. Realizing that Hyer had just spoken the truth he became aware of a movement from Foster that told him that the yellow-haired cowboy had pulled his gun. Katz instinctively reacted. He and Foster fired simultaneously.

Foster was thrown backwards as Katz's bullet slammed into his chest. He seemed to be about to laugh, like a drunken man amused by his own lack of balance. Then the false humour was wiped from his face, his lip rolled up, baring his upper teeth. As Foster flopped lifelessly to the sawdust-covered floor, Katz experienced a sudden pain in his left forearm. The shot fired by Foster hadn't missed him.

Lifting the arm he saw that his sleeve was soaked in blood. At that moment Carmencita hurried up to him, a frown of concern furrowing her brow as she unbuttoned and rolled up his sleeve.

'You can trust me, Jorje,' she assured him. 'I know about these things.'

'The responsibility belongs to all of us, Meredith,' Jeremiah

Sutton said, overhearing Harland berating himself as he came hurrying into the hotel to announce bad news to the little group. 'There has been shooting at the saloon.'

Harland forestalled Aretha by urgently inquiring. 'Who was involved?'

'I have no details. I heard it second-hand from Hank Larwell who came running down the street as I was making my way here. He said that Katz had called out Rob Foster. Things turned nasty then and there was gunplay.'

'Did he know who was hurt?' Aretha interposed.

'Being someone who is frightened of his own shadow even in broad daylight, Hank confessed to me that he rushed out of the place at the sound of the first shot. He heard more gunshots when he was out in the street.'

Hearing this, an animated Harland came to a decision. 'We have to go up there, Jeremiah. Regardless of whatever has happened, is happening, it is fundamentally down to us.'

'I agree,' Sutton said with obvious reservations.

'Forget it,' Aretha spoke up firmly. 'Jorje Katz won't thank you for interfering. He will appreciate your concern, but will not want you involved.'

'But you are equally as troubled as we are, Aretha.' Harland sympathetically protested. 'What if he is seriously injured or, God forbid, dead?'

'That possibility is torturing me. I am frantic with worry,' she acknowledged. 'Nevertheless, you asked Jorje to join in the game, so you must allow him to play it according to his rules.'

'You are an extremely clever lady, Miss Ryland,' Sutton complimented her. 'By becoming involved we would probably exacerbate the situation. It would be wise for us to take your advice.'

Harland sombrely corrected his fellow councillor.

'Presumably the gunplay is over, so there is no situation for us to exacerbate, Jeremiah. We have set ourselves up to run this town in a responsible manner. Deciding to hide away like craven cowards at the first sound of gunshots is no way to set an example.'

Desperately worried, unable to prevent her mind from conjuring up a sequence of images of what may have taken place at the Goldliner, Aretha was aware that the newspaper man had been humbled by Harland's well-chosen words. But she couldn't stay to witness his reaction as she had to hurry away before the tears that were threatening her were shed.

A voice said. 'I'll get the doc here to fix that, Sheriff.'

The speaker was Meredith Harland, who had arrived with Jeremiah Sutton, both looking bewildered at the sight of Katz's bloody arm and McCauley and Foster lying on the floor.

Dropping on to one knee beside Foster, Hyer did a quick examination before looking up at Katz to announce, 'He's dead. That was mighty fine shooting on your part. You got him through the heart, Sheriff.'

'What happened here, Sheriff Katz?' Harland asked.

Wondering how long the two councillors had been in the saloon, Katz was about to remonstrate with them for disobeying his order to keep away, when Carmencita confidently addressed Harland.

'There is no need to fetch Doc Walpole. This is just a flesh wound that I can deal with, and the doc can't do anything for those two *hombres* lying there.'

Seeing the sense of this, Harland said to Katz, 'Get your arm fixed, Sheriff. We will bring "Barber" Shilton to take care of the bodies. You can bring us up to scratch later on what happened here.'

'Before you go,' Katz said quickly, beckoning Hyer to join them and introducing him. 'This is Fernando Hyer.'

'I know who he is,' Harland said bitterly. 'Until a few hours ago he was a prisoner in the Singing River jail.'

'Right now he is my deputy,' Katz announced.

'Tell me that you are jossing, Sheriff.'

'I am serious, Harland, and I am alive. I wouldn't be if it weren't for Fernando.'

Harland responded with a disapproving grunt, but Jeremiah Sutton took charge of the situation. 'Choosing a deputy is your prerogative, Jorje, and from what you say Hyer is a wise choice. Now let the girl fix your arm and we'll have the undertaker take the dead away.'

Uncomfortable as an interloper in his own hotel, Bartholomew Cusick inquired timidly, 'Did I hear right? You say both McCauley and Foster are dead?'

'You heard right, Cusick,' Harland turned away from an impromptu council meeting to reply.

'That worries you, doesn't it Cusick?' Sutton taunted the ex-mayor. 'We know how Clement Foy works. The whole thing from the fracas in the street, the shameful attack on the Reverend Donne, to the carefully staged way that Sheriff Katz was set up in the saloon was obviously a plan worked out by Foy and Sontanna.'

'But Katz is still alive,' Cusick half commented, half asked.

'He is. But he was wounded.'

'Wounded?' Aretha asked the question louder than she had intended. Having just supervised the clearing away after the evening meal, she had joined the group in time to overhear the exchange. A scalp-prickling icy shiver had run through her.

'Not badly, thank heaven,' a sympathetic Sutton assured her.

'Is he at Doc Walpole's?'

'No. He is still at the Goldliner.'

Turning away, wanting to know more, desperately needing to be with Katz, Aretha left the men to their discussion. As she went she heard Zac Horton make a gloomy prediction. 'Foy may not have achieved what he had planned tonight, but he won't stop. He wants to take over this town and the only real obstacle in his way is Sheriff Katz.'

It was a long ride to the Six Bar Six, and a tiring one so late in the day, but Cusick had forced himself to make it. The disappointing news he had heard at his Stageline Hotel had depressed him terribly. He had nurtured high hopes that his unexpected liaison with Clement Foy would quickly return him to an influential position in Singing River. Foy and Santonna, his top hand, had the fight power that he lacked. Yet they had failed miserably that evening, which left him fearful that despite his years of preparation his ultimate dream in life would never become a reality.

On arrival at the ranch his desolation deepened when a smiling Clement Foy greeted him at the door with, 'Great to see you, Bartholomew. Couldn't wait to bring me the good news, eh?'

'There is no good news,' Cusick responded, watching Foy's smile fade.

'What are you saying, Cusick?'

'Danny McCauley and Rob Foster are dead, Clement.'

'Jorje Katz?' Foy questioned, his voice a hoarse whisper.

'Alive and well.' In spite of the implications that answer held for him, Cusick discovered that he derived a perverse pleasure in conveying it to Foy.

A flush of rage darkening his face, Foy muttered. 'I sent boys to do a man's work. I won't make that mistake again.'

'You mean that you will now have Sil Sontanna confront Katz?' Cusick asked hopefully.

'What I intend to do now is no concern of yours,' Foy turned his anger on Cusick.

'But Sontanna will call out Katz?' Cusick risked a double-check.

'Ride out of here right now, Cusick,' Foy ordered menacingly, slamming the ranch house door shut.

Remaining unmoving on the stoop for a minute or two, a disillusioned Cusick then turned to do a slow walk to his horse. His life had taken a drastic downturn. No, that wasn't true. His world had come crashing down around him. A short while ago he had been a largely ignored outsider in the impressive hotel that he owned. Having long ago lost any respect that Aretha Ryland had for him, he now had more need of her than she had of him. Without her to run it the Stageline, his last claim to prominence in Singing River, would be worthless.

Mounting up he rode slowly back towards town, ruing the day he had met Jorje Katz. Now that he had lost Clement Foy he had no allies. By using the cunning and capable Sil Sontanna, Foy had every chance of getting rid of Katz. Then he would be free to depose the self-appointed Meredith Harland and his council, take over the town, and appoint his own mayor and sheriff. Bartholomew Cusick would not figure anywhere in Foy's plans.

He wasn't going to let that happen. It would be necessary to act fast to foil Foy's objective, and it would cost him a considerable sum of money, but he was determined to do it. Preliminary ideas began to present themselves, and by the time he had reached Singing River's perimeter he had perfected in his mind the first move he must make.

*

Pausing to look over the batwing doors into the Goldliner Saloon, Aretha struggled to find the courage to go in. It wasn't really courage that she required; what she needed was a method to overcome revulsion. She detested the noise, the stench, the people, and the immoral ambience of the place. Even so, her angst over Katz's safety was forcing her to go forwards. Taking a deep breath wasn't an option in this fetid atmosphere. Concentrating on the thought of being with Jorje Katz, she pushed open the doors and went in.

Overwhelmed for a moment, she saw everything all at once but none of it registered. Then her panic eased and she was aware of the lecherous stares of men, and the suspicious angry glances of girls fearing competition. Then nothing mattered to her when she saw Katz standing at the bar and made her way towards him. She came to a sudden halt as she saw a girl beside Katz. She was smiling up at him as she undid his shirt sleeve and checked on his bandaged forearm.

Recognizing Carmencita and disappointed by her closeness to Katz, but relieved that he had not seen her come into the saloon, Aretha did a speedy about turn and went quickly out into the street.

A voice coming out of the darkness behind startled her. 'Hello, Aretha, what are you doing in this neck of the woods so late in the night?'

Comforted by discovering it was Doc Walpole who had called to her, she waited for him to catch up with her. With false cheerfulness she countered with, 'Before answering that I need to know what you are doing off limits, Doc?'

'My Good Samaritan act, my dear. I have taken Isaac Donne to his home.'

'He is well again now, Doc?'

'As well as can be expected after so traumatic an experience,' Walpole assured her, stopping under a naphtha light mounted on the corner of the saloon and taking her arm to turn her towards him. Looking intently at her for a long while, he spoke at last. 'I thought I saw tears glistening in those lovely eyes of yours, my dear Aretha. You have taken some hard knocks since you came to Singing River, and I have admired the stoical way you have handled yourself. It would take something extremely drastic to make a woman like you weep, so tell me what is troubling you?'

'Nothing, Doc, honestly.'

'Honesty is one of your many virtues, so tell me what ails you, Aretha. I saw you come out of the Goldliner and there is only one reason for you to visit such a place. Has he been badly hurt?'

'No.'

'But he has hurt you?'

'We haven't even spoken, so the answer to that is no.'

'You can't fool an oldster like me, Aretha,' the old doctor cautioned her. 'Have you left someone in charge of the hotel?'

'Miguel is taking care of the place.'

'He's a good lad,' Walpole acknowledged, slipping an arm around her waist. 'As a physician I advise you of the benefits to be derived from unburdening a troubled soul. We will go to my place and talk while enjoying cups of the best Arbuckle's coffee.'

'You are not watching your back, Jorje,' Hyer quietly issued a warning as he joined Katz at the bar.

Apart from a brief lull immediately following the shooting of McCauley and Foster, the wild, noisy celebration in the Goldliner Saloon had lost none of its momentum. Consequently, Katz, having been vigilant all evening, corrected his young deputy. 'There hasn't been a hint of trouble since the earlier shooting.'

'Not that sort of danger, Sheriff. I'm talking of the calico kind.'

'You'd better explain yourself, Fernando.'

'It probably doesn't come under a deputy's duties,' Hyer said with an indifferent shrug.

'It sure does now since you brought it up,' Katz told him. 'Say your piece.'

'Well,' Hyer hesitantly began, 'while you were in the company of that Mexican girl a real lady walked into this den of unwashed humanity. She had both beauty and breeding, real class.'

'If that was so, what was she doing in here, Fernando?'

'That occurred to me. Such a woman should not even pass by within half a mile of the doors of this *bordello.* I was shocked to see Aretha Ryland walk in.'

'How is it you recognized her and know her name?' Katz was incredulous.

'I saw her once in New York. She was an actress performing on the stage in a great play called *Shenandoah.*'

'New York, theatres!' Katz exclaimed. 'You are a man of many parts, Fernando.'

'Maybe,' Hyer shrugged. 'But I sure am not the equal of a man who has a woman like Aretha Ryland coming into this honkeytonk looking for me.'

'We don't know that I was the reason she came in here,' Katz pointed out.

'That is true, Jorje but the fact that she didn't stay long after she saw you with your strumpet seems like real proof to me.'

Though irritated by Hyer's reference to Carmencita as a whore, Katz let it pass. Uppermost in his mind was profound regret. Hyer was absolutely correct in saying there was only one reason for Aretha to come to the saloon, and that was concern for him. Seeing him with Carmencita, who had done nothing more but to tend the wound in his arm, had made her leave immediately.

Perhaps the solution to the problem was for him to go to the hotel and explain exactly what she had seen on entering the saloon. Considering making this move, Katz cancelled the idea after grasping that it would be wrong both for Aretha and for him to take their relationship further at that time. His killing of two Six Bar Six men that evening meant that he now had a war on his hands that would require him not only to be continuously ready for action, but also to be in the firing line at all times. To get closer to Aretha now would be to cause her anxiety both day and night. He was rescued from his gloomy thoughts by a nudge from Hyer who pointed to his empty glass.

'You ready for another, Jorje.'

With his mind made up it took only a brief moment to answer. 'Yep.'

'I have never met a man like him,' Aretha emphasized to the old doctor as they sat in comfortable chairs in a cosy room drinking coffee.

'You have never said a truer word, my dear,' he agreed, smiling fondly at Aretha. 'He is a rarity, a one-off. That should encourage you, not daunt you.'

'Though I know that you are much wiser than me, Doc, I can't agree with you on that. Jorje has never settled anywhere during his lifetime. That makes it highly unlikely that he will do so now or at any other time in the future.'

'Now it is my turn to disagree,' Walpole said with a little apologetic smile. 'Even a man like Katz can change when he meets the right woman.'

'I think he has met her in the Goldliner Saloon,' Aretha disconsolately voiced her opinion.

'Carmencita? I think not, my dear. A most fetching young woman, that cannot be denied, but she is a saloon girl nonetheless.'

'Even so, she fits into his life far better than I ever could, Doc.'

'His life as he has always known it, not as he now wants it to be. I am confident that I can prove you wrong, Aretha.'

Interested but doubtful, she asked. 'How could you do that?'

'As a student of human nature I have come to know you well, Aretha, and though Katz is the type who is an enigma to the majority, I have learned much about him in a very short time.'

'But he is still an enigma to me, Doc. I can't see how I can ever get through the invisible barrier he has placed around himself.'

'The opportunity to do so won't occur until the battle for supremacy in Singing River is won,' the old doctor replied in a smug but far from unpleasant manner. 'At that time the chance of a proper and lasting relationship between the two of you will present itself.'

'But surely what he will go through between now and then will harden his attitude towards life even more, Doc?'

Pouring more coffee for them both he denied her supposition with a shake of his head. 'Every hard man I have ever known has mellowed at some time later in his life, and I am confident that Jorje won't prove to be an exception.'

'How can you be so sure of that?' Aretha questioned, wanting to believe.

'Because he is a caring man. He became very fond of little Estelle. When she was well enough I took her back home and the Edwards told me that Katz had called earlier to ensure that everything was in order and that she would be safe. You see, the Edwards' homestead is under threat from several directions because it has water, a precious commodity without which no big rancher like Clement Foy can expand.'

'That was kind of him, Doc.'

'That is the sort of man that he is. He even asked if it would be in order for him to visit occasionally to see the girl.'

'That would be difficult for anyone to believe when meeting Jorje for the first time. But when you get to know him—'

'As you and I have,' Walpole cut in.

'That's right. Then it is easy to accept.'

'All that you must do is be patient, my dear.'

'But he will be spending a lot of time at the Goldliner, Doc,' Aretha mused. 'He will be in Carmencita's company much more often than he will see me.'

'Saloon girls belong in his past, whereas you are a part of his future.'

'Is there anything else you can say to persuade me to believe that, Doc?'

'Nothing further is necessary, my dear.'

Will Olaf didn't amount to much. He hadn't since achieving modest fame as a horseman during the brief lifetime of the Pony Express. That fast-fading reputation was good enough for the needs of Bartholomew Cusick, who had reached a decision on returning home after his frustrating late-night visit to Clement Foy at the Six Bar Six. Priding himself on being a man of action, he forsook the comfort of his bed to set in motion the opening tactic in his fight back to prominence in the Singing River community.

It was close to midnight as he made his way to the derelict

Rest and Welcome hotel, which now provided free lodgings for Olaf and others of his low class. The lateness of the hour didn't worry Cusick, for whom sleep would be impossible before he put his strategy on course, and would probably be just as impossible afterwards.

Being of a pernickety nature, he became nauseous on visiting several stinking rooms before finding Olaf lying under a foul smelling sack in a filthy cubicle. Nervous to the point of panic caused by being awakened, Olaf took several minutes to calm down sufficiently for Cusick to enlighten him as to the reason for his visit.

'I have a little job for you, Olaf. I want you to ride to Santa Fe.'

'I ain't got a horse,' Olaf protested.

'Land sakes! I'll provide you with a horse,' an exasperated Cusick shouted angrily.

'It'll cost yuh.'

'I'll pay for the gosh-darn horse.'

'I mean you will have to pay me.'

'I will pay you well for what is a simple task,' Cusick assured him. 'I need you to take a written message to a man named Jack Poole. I'll tell you where to find him.'

'All I have to do is hand the message over?'

'That's all. But when you do you must tell him that I insist it must be Johnny Lyng that he sends here to me. Can you remember that name?'

'That's easy to remember. Everyone has heard of Johnny Lyng.'

'Good,' a satisfied Cusick acknowledged. 'Now get on you feet. I want you to start out right away.'

'Now? It's the middle of the night!'

Walking to the door of the room, Cusick turned to ask. 'Do you want to earn money or don't you?'

'I need the *dinero*.'

'Then get moving, Olaf. Meet me down at Al Petain's stables. I'll have a horse saddled and ready for you.'

Relieved to be outside in the cool, fresh air of night, Cusick was contented. There wasn't one gunslinger in the West who could match Johnny Lyng on the draw, and that included Jorje Katz. Lyng would come at a high price, but he would be well worth it.

Walking slowly home he looked cheerfully up at the starry sky. The rebuff he had received from Clement Foy was largely forgotten as he focused on a bright future in which he would regain his former position in Singing River for which he had worked so long and so hard.

EIGHT

A few short days had brought a welcome change to Singing River. Katz and his deputy patrolled the streets each evening, letting the ranch-hands who arrived in small groups know that the law would be strictly enforced. This strategy served to remind ranch-hands of the gunplay and the resultant loss of life that occurred on the recent pay night, causing them to return to their ranches to warn that the old pay night celebrations belonged in the past and would never return.

The tight grip that Katz had on the town launched Meredith Harland's council as an effective body, enabling it to make general improvements to the local facilities that pleased the townsfolk. Thankful that the self-interest regime of Bartholomew Cusick had come to an end, Singing River had taken on a new lease of life. However, there was an underlying fear that the powerful Clement Foy would at any time make a takeover move. Most accepted that it was bound to happen and wondered what chance Katz and Hyer, his young deputy, had if Foy was to release the might of the Six Bar Six against the town.

This possibility was constantly on Aretha's mind, and she broached the subject to Katz as she sat with him in the Stageline Hotel while he ate his evening meal. She had noticed that since the gunplay at the Goldliner Saloon he had been noticeably reserved when with her, although his manner was as polite and caring as ever. Not long before she had sensed that it had crossed his mind that he and she might well have a future together. She now suspected that in the dangerous situation that had developed in Singing River, he was resigned to the very real possibility that he had no future.

'You say that Fernando is a skilled gunfighter, Jorje,' she attempted to put her worry as subtlety as possible. 'I don't doubt that he is a capable young man, but that doesn't alter the fact that there are only two of you. If Foy's men should ride into town in force you would stand no chance.'

'Whatever else Clement Foy may be he is a proud man, Aretha. That being so, I don't see him openly making a mass attack on the town with his gunslingers. To do so would rob him of his reputation as an upright citizen. The same applies to Sil Sontanna. He is one of the old gunfighters who prides himself on being quick on the draw and with the courage to face any man fair and square.'

'Perhaps Sontanna won't be allowed to maintain that stance. He works for Clement Foy, who despite his pride and his Bible-bashing is an unscrupulous man,' Aretha pointed out.

'You know what the Good Book says about pride coming before the fall, Aretha.'

'That's as maybe. It would take an awful lot to cause Clement Foy to fall. You know how I feel about Cusick. I am every bit as glad as anyone to see him go down, but he didn't wield the frightening power that Foy has.'

'You wouldn't welcome Cusick back as he was.'

'I wouldn't wish it to happen, but I would feel easier than I do now.'

'Don't be fooled into thinking Cusick has given up. He is a cunning man and not the type to come back with all guns blazing.'

'If he did it would be someone else's guns blazing, and Cusick would be hiding behind whoever it is.'

'That's what I was trying to point out,' Katz said, giving her a smile. 'You are very astute, Aretha.'

'I often wish that I wasn't,' Aretha smiled a false smile to accept his compliment. 'At a time such as this it would be better to remain ignorant. You believe that it might not be only Foy who causes trouble, but that Cusick may well have a few nasty tricks up his sleeve?'

'It is possible. Whatever happens, whoever starts anything, I will take care of you,' Katz promised.

'It isn't me that I'm worried about. It is your safety that bothers me both day and night.'

'Would you have me ride away, Aretha?'

'I know better than to even suggest such a thing to you,' she complimented him.

Made uncomfortable by the admiration she was showing for him, Katz forced himself to gently advise, 'Regardless of how this ends, I won't be remaining here in Singing River, Aretha.'

'It seems that you are giving me a message of some kind, Jorje.'

This was more of a question than a statement. Hating himself for doing so, he left it unanswered, aware that his silence would have her understand that he didn't want her to become emotionally involved with him.

Standing up, he said lightly. 'It is time to patrol the mean streets of Singing River.'

With uncharacteristic boldness, Aretha got to her feet to kiss him lightly on the cheek before he could turn to leave.

*

There were two riders approaching. They came out of an early morning haze at a slow pace that added to Joel Edwards' apprehension. Having anticipated trouble ever since Doc Walpole had brought his daughter back home, he was convinced that it was about to happen. Even so, he hesitated to call a warning to Heather through the open cabin doorway, not wanting to cause her unnecessary alarm should it transpire that the two horsemen were not a threat.

He changed his mind as the two riders came closer and he recognized them as Six Bar Six hands. The tall, lean one with a hawkish face was Glen Fowler, while the other was the stocky, powerfully built Ray Wilding. Both of them were regarded as dangerous troublemakers in the district, and particularly in town. Recognizing them, Joel was glad that he hadn't alerted his wife. He preferred for her to remain inside the cabin while vicious scalywags like these two were present.

Reining up at a distance of a few feet from him, both riders dismounted. Their walk up to him was aggressive and their arrogant demeanour distinctly menacing.

'Clement Foy asked us to call and check that everything is all right with you all here,' Wilding announced.

'Why would Foy be interested in our welfare?'

With a shrug, Fowler answered Edwards' question. 'As everyone knows, Clement Foy is a God-fearing, law-abiding man who likes to be certain that everything is in order. He cares about people, even a nester like you. Having said that, Mr Foy sure hates people squatting on the range.'

'I'm no squatter. I bought this place fair and square,' Joel protested angrily, aware that his wife was now standing in the doorway with their daughter clinging to her skirts.

'That ain't exactly true,' Glen Fowler argued. 'Seems like

you have failed to keep up the payments. I guess you are as poor as a hind-tit calf, and that don't fit in with Mr Foy's idea of how things should be on the range.'

'That is none of Foy's business.'

'Mr Foy is doing nothing other than exercising the gosh darned right to make it his business, Edwards. Bartholomew Cusick is right worried about his financial position with you and has asked Mr Foy to help him out where his money and the like is concerned.'

'That's how it is, Edwards,' Wilding joined in. 'Clement was only too willing to assist. He has been a regular and satisfied customer at Cusick's bank for a right considerable time, and is real keen to help him get the money that you owes him. That don't mean that we've been sent here today to take money from you that you probably don't have. You see, our boss also sees it as putting everyone hereabouts down if he allows you to let a place like this go to rack and ruin.'

'Clement Foy or no one else will find anything wrong with this place,' Joel proudly said.

'I don't agree with that, do you, Glen?' the stocky man asked his companion.

'I sure as shootin' don't, Ray,' Fowler responded, indicating the Edwards' milk cow. 'Look at that dogie, riddled with disease. That's the sort of thing that Clement Foy don't want spreading to his or any other rancher herds in the district.'

'You're danged right he don't,' Wilding agreed, drawing his six-shooter as he told Joel, 'This is the sort of thing we've been sent here to put right, Edwards.'

'Don't!' Joel shouted as the stocky cowhand started walking towards the cow.

As the Foy man kept walking, Joel ran to the cabin doorway, reaching in with the intention of picking up his shotgun. It wasn't there.

He desperately asked, 'Where's my scattergun, Heather?'

'I hid it away, Joel.'

'Tell me where it is!' a frantic Joel shouted as he turned his head to see Wilding holding his six-shooter against the cow's head just above and between its eyes. 'He's going to shoot our cow.'

'If I give you your gun he will shoot you,' a weeping Heather told him.

She had just spoken the last word as Wilding pulled the trigger, and Estelle screamed loudly, burying her face in her mother's skirt as the cow shuddered, took a bent-legged little step sideways before losing its balance and falling to the ground to lie still.

'Well lookee here,' Wilding remarked as he walked over to where the Edwards' horse stood in a small corral. 'Looks to me like this jughead's every bit as sick as that cow.'

'Couldn't look that stupid if it wasn't,' Fowler concurred, moving to join his companion.

'Get away from that horse!' Joel shouted, running across to the two men.

'Joel, don't!' his wife called, but she was too late.

As Joel reached him, Wilding reversed the gun in his hand. Holding the barrel he swung the six-shooter to swipe a hard blow with the butt to Joel's head. Followed by a weeping Estelle, Heather ran across to her husband as he collapsed. Dropping to her knees she sobbed as she cradled his injured head, his blood running thickly down her bare arm.

Screaming and seemingly about to flee, Estelle then moved tentatively closer to her parents, averting her gaze from her stricken father before clinging to her distraught mother.

Exchanging grins, Fowler and Wilding turned away to concentrate on the horse. Still holding his gun, Wilding humorously remarked as he first pointed to Edwards and then to the animal. 'One down, one to go.'

Amused by this, Fowler's raucous laughter completely drowned out the sound of Heather's and her daughter's crying.

Reaching the crest of a hill, Jorje Katz reined up to look through a misty haze down the long slope leading to the Edwards' homestead. He hadn't intended to ride out there that morning, and was prepared to discover that he was wasting his time. But he had been uneasy since Carmencita had come to stand near to him at the bar in the Goldliner the previous night. She hadn't looked in his direction, so no one would have known that she was speaking to him.

'I overheard something that I think you would want to know, Jorje,' she had told him.

'Your help is welcome, Carmencita,' he had said, following her example of disguising the fact that they were conversing.

'It's about the Edwards family. Foy wants them off their homestead and he's planning to start causing them problems.'

'When will this happen?'

Katz had been alarmed. Although Joel Edwards had the courage to defend his wife and child and their home, he was a farmer not a fighting man. Consequently, there was no way that he could offer any resistance to Foy and his plan. Yet he would try, and would likely die in the attempt.

'I'm sorry, Jorje, I was unable to learn that.'

'You don't have to apologize. It is very brave of you to risk your own safety by warning me of this, Carmencita.'

'I told you when we first met that you would need the help of someone, and that someone is me.'

'I am lucky to have you with me, in more ways than one. But please promise that you will take care.'

'You have my promise, Jorje. I have plans for us when this is all over.'

Carmencita's intentions where he was concerned had not caused him to worry but the uncertainty of when Foy would start harassing the Edwards' meant that Katz couldn't rest until he had visited the homestead to make sure that all was well.

He was about to move on down the gradient when the piercing shriek of a child's scream came to him on the still morning air. Knowing that it had to have been Estelle who had screamed, dread made him immobile for a split second. Then he dug in the spurs, pulled hard left on the reins to have his horse gallop into the thickly wooded area that ran down the side of the trail to the homestead.

Risking his own life and that of his panicking horse, he weaved around the trees and rode at a reckless speed through brushwood. Reaching level ground he reined up some thirty feet from the homestead. Pulling his rifle from its saddle scabbard as he dismounted in one smooth movement, he then made his silent way to the rear of the cabin.

Hearing the voices of men and laughter, he moved stealthily along the side of the log building. Peering cautiously around the corner he saw Heather and Estelle Edwards on their knees beside the inert body of Joel. Two men wearing stained Levi's, one tall and thin, the other of medium height and broad-shouldered, stood with their backs to him facing a horse. As he watched, the stocky man pressed his six-gun against the head of the horse.

Bringing up his rifle, Katz took aim at the right shoulder of the shorter man and fired. The force of the rifle bullet spun the man round several times, the gun flying harmlessly from his hand. Facing Katz with a surprised expression on his face, he clapped a hand to his shoulder before doing a quarter turn and collapsing over the top rail of the corral.

The second man turned in Katz's direction, about to go for his holstered gun. But Katz was running towards him at speed, getting to him before he had the chance to clear leather, and driving the stock of his rifle hard against the side of the man's head.

Splashed with blood before the man fell, Katz went quickly to the two horses hitched nearby. Taking a lariat from the saddle of each, he came back, first to the tall man who was then sitting with his back against a well, groaning as he massaged his bleeding shoulder in a pointless attempt at easing the pain.

Placing his foot in the middle of the man's back Katz half pushed, half kicked him face down on the ground. Uncaring about increasing his agony, Katz pulled the man's arm with the wounded shoulder behind him then reached to do the same with the other arm before tying the wrists together with the rope. Then he moved the rope down to secure the man's legs tightly together.

Kicking away the six-gun that lay in the dust, Katz then moved to the stocky man who was unconscious. Taking his gun from the holster he threw it far off across the yard before using the second lariat to bind his arms and legs.

Hurrying across to where the woman and child sat on the ground beside the still unconscious Joel Edwards, Katz gently eased them both back on to their feet. Seeing a bucket of water close by, he removed his neckerchief to soak it in the water. Going back to kneel beside Joel he lay the wet cloth against his forehead. Patiently waiting until Joel's eyes flickered and then opened, he went back to rinse the blood from the neckerchief before soaking it again and returning to wash the blood, first from Joel's face and then his hair.

'Do you want me to ride to the Edwards' place and find out what's happened, boss?'

Sil Sontanna asked the question as he stood beside an anxious Clement Foy looking to the trail leading to a distant hill. Fowler and Wilding were overdue, yet there was still no sign of any horseman as far as the eye could see.

Foy shook his head. 'No. The boys are probably having fun harassing Edwards. Give it another hour, Sil. That squatter couldn't do them any harm.'

'But Katz could,' Sontanna suggested grimly.

'Katz is in town,' Foy countered.

'Katz could be anywhere. Right now he could be out at that homestead. Never underestimate that *hombre*, Clem.'

'I reckon as how it's you that has to bear that in mind, Sil, as it's certain that you will have to face the guy sometime soon.'

'I know that. I'll be ready,' Sontanna assured his boss.

Having got Joel into a chair and had Heather produce a medicine box, Katz had cleansed the wound, applied iodine and bandaged the homesteader's head. Then he had made broth and cut bread to feed the parents and child. All three seemed to be recovering from their ordeal suffered at the hands of the Six Bar Six men, although Estelle occasionally sobbed as she mourned the death of Maisie the cow. All three of them became sad when Katz prepared to leave.

Although Joel was unsteady on his feet, he came outside to join Heather in expressing their thanks to Katz for his help. Cheering up, Estelle giggled as Katz bodily picked up the now conscious but still tightly bound Wilding and threw him face down across the saddle of his horse. Katz then grasped the spare length of rope dangling from the lariat binding Wilding's legs, and used it to secure him to his horse.

Repeating the same routine with Fowler, who cried out in agony as Katz's rough movements boosted the pain from his injured shoulder, Katz hitched the reins of Fowler's horse to the rear of Wilding's saddle.

Going to where the Edwards family stood watching, he sat on his heels in front of Estelle and held her hands, saying, 'No need for any more crying, Estelle. I will make sure that you have another cow very soon.'

'Thank you,' she said, reaching out with her thin arms to hug him.

Patting her on the head as he stood, he shook hands with Joel, who expressed his thanks. 'We will be in your debt forever more, and there is no way that I can properly thank you.'

'You owe me nothing, and I need no thanks for dealing with varmints like this,' Katz replied as he gestured towards the two men tied to their horses.

Heather took a step forward to lightly place a hand on his upper arm and said a quiet, 'Thank you.'

Taking the reins of Wilding's horse in his hand, Katz swung up into the saddle. He moved off then, trailing the other two horses. He did not look back.

'You will want to see this, Aretha!'

Doc Walpole's excited shout had Aretha hurry to the open door where he stood. Side by side they watched Katz ride at a walking pace down the far side of the street leading two horses, each of which had a man tied across the saddle. Looking neither to left nor to right, Katz passed them by and continued on down the street. A group of men and saloon girls had come out of the Goldliner, Aretha noticed that

Carmencita was among them, and many folk along the street had come to stand in doorways, fascinated by the strange and somehow eerie little procession.

'Are those men dead?' Aretha fearfully inquired.

'I would say that whether or not they are is inconsequential,' the old doctor reasoned. 'They are doubtless Six Bar Six men so, dead or alive, there will be hell to pay. Clement Foy has already lost men to Jorje Katz and he is going to be mad as a peeled rattler. My guess is that there will be gunsmoke in Singing River before this night is out.'

They could see Fernando Hyer waiting at the jailhouse door as Katz reined up and dismounted. Hyer came out across the boardwalk to help Katz untie one man and carry him inside. They came back out to untie the other man.

'They look like bodies to me, Doc.'

'Could be,' Walpole half agreed with Aretha as the two lawmen carried the second man into the jailhouse. 'Even I can't be sure from this distance.'

It was close to midnight when the rumble of hoof beats warned Katz and Hyer of the approach of many riders. They were sitting sipping rye whisky. Fowler and Wilding were locked in separate cells, Hyer having gone to the hotel earlier to fetch Doc Walpole down to dig the rifle bullet from Fowler's shoulder and bandage the wound.

'Aretha will want to know what's been happening, Jorje,' the old doc had mentioned when about to leave having completed his doctoring. 'What do I tell her?'

'Just that everything is fine and there's nothing to worry about, Doc,' Katz replied, aware that it didn't satisfy the doctor, and it definitely wouldn't suffice as an answer for Aretha.

Now, an hour later, he placed his glass on the table and

spoke casually to Hyer. 'I reckon we are about to have company.'

'Should I get out some extra glasses?' Hyer wryly inquired.

'Perhaps it might be best to check your handgun,' Katz advised as the sound of horses coming to a halt and men dismounting came from outside.

'How do you intend to handle this, Jorje?'

'Diplomatically.'

'I won't need my handgun then,' Hyer commented understatedly.

'I wouldn't count on that,' Katz answered ironically as a shout came from outside.

'Are you there, Katz?'

'I'm here.'

'This is Sil Sontanna. You have two of my men in there.'

'Not so, Sontanna. But I do have two of Clement Foy's men locked up.'

'Don't try to get smart, Katz,' Sontanna shouted a warning. 'I am foreman at the Six Bar Six.'

'That cuts no ice with me, Sontanna. Fetch Foy here.'

'I am here, Katz,' Clement Foy's raised voice reached Katz and Hyer. 'I am told you are holding two of my men.'

'That's right, Foy.'

'Then release both of them immediately.'

'I don't take orders from you or anyone else,' Katz answered.

'You had better start taking them right now, Katz. I have Sil Sontanna and twenty gun hands out here.'

'They aren't much good to you out there, seeing as how your two men are in here.'

'I'll give you ten seconds to open the door, Katz, otherwise we will smash it down.'

'Do that and I'll guarantee that the first ten men coming

in will die, Foy.'

Several dragging minutes of silence followed. The only sounds to be heard were the occasional jingle of a harness as a horse shook its head and snorted.

'Foy is testing our nerves by building up the tension, Jorje,' Hyer commented.

'Is he getting to you, kid?'

'Cut out that kid stuff, or I will walk out through that door and throw in my lot with the other side.'

'Open the door and you'll fall back in riddled with bullets,' Katz predicted. 'I'm sorry about the kid bit. It was a slip of the tongue.'

'Most probably this situation is getting to your nerves,' Hyer said in jest.

'Then I had better do something about it,' Katz said. He shouted to Foy, 'I'm willing to discuss the two prisoners with you, Foy. Give me your word that you'll move your men back, and no tricks will be tried, and I will open the door and let you in. But only you. Come alone, or we will gun down you and anyone you bring with you.'

There was a pause, and then Foy called, 'You have my word.'

'Move over to the left side of the door, Fernando, standing back about six feet,' Katz instructed before going to the door and sliding the bolts.

Obeying, Hyer drew his gun while Katz opened the door ajar then walked several paces backwards and reached for his gun, calling, 'The door is open, Foy. Come on in.'

Some tense moments passed before Katz and Hyer heard footfalls on the boardwalk. Then a foot pushed the door inwards and Foy appeared, framed in the doorway. He wasn't wearing a gunbelt and held his hands up surrender-style, palms facing forwards. Uncertainty had painted a faint smile on his lined, stern face.

'You can put your hands down and step inside,' Katz said, ready to move round behind the rancher to kick the door shut.

As Foy moved forwards two men stepped into the doorway behind him, one each side, both holding guns.

Reacting instantly, Katz and Hyer fired. One of the gunmen was knocked backwards out on to the boardwalk, while the other pitched forwards on to his face just inside the door, staining the floorboards with blood. Covered by Hyer, Katz moved at lightning speed. Shoving his right foot under the prone body on the floor, he executed what was part kick, part leverage to move it outside. Kicking the door closed he bolted it with his left hand while, still holding his six-gun in his right hand, he caught Foy a heavy backhanded blow that sent him backwards to crash against the wall.

Holstering his gun, he caught Foy by the lapels of his jacket to prevent him from collapsing, and threw him into a chair.

'Are you all right, Clem?' Sontanna's voice called from outside.

Barely conscious, Foy hadn't heard his foreman's inquiry. Attempting to revive him, Katz slapped him hard across the face backwards and forwards, again and again. All this achieved was to have Foy peer groggily at Katz through half-closed eyes.

Grabbing a jug of water from a nearby table, Hyer tossed the contents into Foy's face. This brought the rancher round just as Sontanna repeated his call.

'Are you all right, Clem?'

'Answer him,' Katz snarled, grabbing Foy's coat to shake him vigorously.

'I'm fine, Sil, don't worry. I will be back out there with you soon,' the rancher managed to croak. Then he said to Katz. 'I don't suppose that will happen.'

'I should shoot you after you pulled that trick, Foy.'

'There's no need for that,' Foy weakly protested. 'You have just killed two more of my men. I have had enough. You let me walk out of here and me and my men will ride away. You have my word on that.'

'I had your word not ten minutes ago,' Katz retorted. 'I'm calling the shots now, and I'm offering you two options. Option one is that Hyer and me take you to the door. Standing each side of you, we'll open the door and blast away at your men.'

'They would have to fire back!' Foy was aghast. 'I would be killed.'

'Rough justice,' Katz stated.

'I sure would like to hear the second option, Jorje,' Hyer commented, causing a nervous Foy to signal with a nod that he too wanted to hear it.

'It's simple. We negotiate and both you and me stick to what we agree.'

'I'll give you my w—' Foy began, cutting short when he saw the expression on Katz's face.

'This is my offer, Foy. I give you one of the men we have locked up back there. That will be the one with the wounded shoulder, so you can do the doctoring. You take him and that bunch of renegades outside and leave town. But there are conditions attached. They are that you leave the Edwards in peace and you immediately replace the milk cow that your men killed.'

'I am prepared to keep to that agreement but not as it now stands,' Foy replied. 'All I get in return is one of my men?'

'You will have the second man back when I learn that a cow has been delivered to the Edwards' homestead.'

'In that case, we have a deal, Katz.'

NINE

Katz and Carmencita reined up on the edge of a plateau. Not dismounting, they sat together enjoying the magnificent view. The ground in front of them swept down in a wooded slope to a seemingly infinite stretch of verdant grassland. A late afternoon sun painted the summer sky a brilliant orange. There was an unearthly stillness that brought about some kind of change of consciousness that had them both relaxed and unspeaking.

The day hadn't been the one that Katz had planned. While in the Goldliner Saloon last evening he had mentioned to Carmencita that he was riding out to the Edwards' homestead in the morning. His visit was mainly to check if Foy had replaced the cow and that the family had suffered no further harassment.

When he had arrived at the stables that morning he had found Carmencita there. Wearing a white Stetson and looking even more attractive than when she was in the saloon, she had hired a palomino horse. Puzzled by her being there, and wondering why she had rented a horse, he hadn't had long to wait before she had enlightened him.

'I am hoping you will let me ride with you today, Jorje,' she had archly explained, giving his magnificent black stallion an envious glance. 'I am so tired of seeing nothing more than this one-horse town every day, and the inside of that horrible saloon every night.'

The idea of her joining him had held strong appeal, and he had agreed, convincing himself that his motive was recognition that he was in her debt due to her having risked her own safety by helping him since he had come to Singing River.

His reward had been a most enjoyable day. Surprising Katz, the Edwards had taken to Carmencita despite her being a saloon girl. An excited Estelle had been eager to have her meet 'Maisie 2', the new cow.

Carmencita broke the silence between her and Katz now as they sat getting pleasure from the view.

'Thank you for taking me along today, Jorje. I have had a really lovely time. Never having a family of my own, the hours I spent with that lovely little girl and her parents mean a lot to me. I shall remember every minute for the rest of my life.'

'I am very pleased to hear that, Carmencita.'

'The difficulty comes with having to return to my regular life,' she wistfully said, looking out over the vast space. 'I know it's a daydream, but how would you feel if right this moment we could ride off down there and live as the Comanche, the Apache, and other tribes once lived? If we owned nothing but a tipi, some weapons for hunting, and the freedom of the prairies?'

'I wouldn't hesitate for one moment,' Katz replied. 'But, as you said, it is a daydream. Now we have to head back into what is called civilization.'

'Then can we please ride slowly? I want to savour every last minute of this wonderful day, Jorje.'

Moved by her sadness, Katz could only give a nod of assent as he reined his horse about and moved off.

*

Aretha was unhappy at the sight of Katz and Carmencita riding unhurriedly back into town. Though normally unprejudiced, she found comfort by dismissing Carmencita as a saloon girl. Even so, she was a woman, a beautiful one, with a wildness about her that made Katz and her seem a perfect match.

'Ah, Katz is back. I was expecting him to have gone alone.'

Turning her head, Aretha saw that Hyer had stepped out of the hotel to stand beside her on the boardwalk. She heard herself ask anxiously. 'Back from where?'

'He rode out to the Edwards' place this morning, and it looks like he had company.'

'Perhaps they happened to meet just outside of town after coming from different directions,' she supposed, hoping to convince herself, but failing to do so.

Hyer didn't answer as they watched the two riders dismount outside of Al Petain's stables and lead their horses in. Aretha found herself waiting for Hyer to speak. In the short time since Katz had introduced him to her she had found the young gunslinger to be well-educated and knowledgeable. It was difficult for her to adjust to finding those qualities in a young man leading Hyer's kind of life, especially since a short time ago he had discussed with her a play in which she had appeared in New York.

He proved his intelligence then by making a remark that revealed that he knew why she had been watching Katz and Carmencita: 'Mark Antony and Cleopatra.'

'All that I can see is a sheriff and a saloon girl,' Aretha couldn't help contesting his Shakespearean assessment of the couple.

'That's because logic flees when we fall in love, Aretha,' Hyer advised. 'The only hope for a woman who wants Jorje Katz is to first lasso him and then hogtie him. I am speaking figuratively, of course.'

'You are an intelligent man, Fernando, but you are as blind as a post hole where romance is concerned,' Aretha chided him. 'I have no interest in Jorje Katz other than as a friend. I hope that I have made that plain to you.'

'Maybe, maybe not,' Hyer said with a shrug.

Reluctantly accepting that she had lost the argument, Aretha knew that she deserved to because she had been lying to both Hyer and to herself.

'I have honoured our agreement, Katz,' Clement Foy announced as he walked into the jailhouse.

Taking a bunch of keys from the table and tossing them to Hyer who lounged in a chair, Katz said. 'Fetch Wilding out here, Fernando.'

'You have learned that I am a man of my word,' a pleased Foy said with a smile.

'Not exactly,' Katz calmly answered. 'I happened to call on Joel Edwards this morning and found him milking a cow.'

'I can't say that your humour is appreciated, Katz,' Foy said, carefully concealing his annoyance. 'Nevertheless, you can rely on my pledge that the Edwards will receive no further pressure from me.'

The conversation lapsed then as Hyer returned with Wilding, who walked over to stand beside Foy. Glancing briefly at him, Foy said, 'Wait for me outside. I won't be long.'

When the door had closed behind Wilding, Katz asked, 'You have your man back, so is there something else, Foy?'

'I would like to speak with you,' Foy answered, looking significantly in Hyer's direction.

'Go ahead,' Katz invited. 'Hyer stays.'

Hesitating on hearing this, Foy then began speaking. 'It is not sensible for either you or for me for us to continue at cross purposes.'

'We don't have to,' Katz reasoned. 'The answer is simple if we take a look at the situation. I am the John Law here, so if you and your outfit don't break any laws there is no possibility for any hostility between us.'

'That was the point I was going to make, Katz. I am a businessman who will defend any threat to my business with force. Having said that, I am also a man with strong religious convictions. I regard you as a man of principle who is an asset for the good folk of Singing River and the surrounding district. There has been strife and uncertainty hereabouts for too long. Peace is long overdue in Singing River.'

'What are you saying, Foy?'

'What I believe is a most reasonable and workable solution to what ails this territory. I am prepared to ensure that no Six Bar Six man will ever again seriously trouble any local individual or group. That, of course, includes you.'

'What are you asking in return?'

'Nothing other than if any of my men should infringe the law, then you will react strictly according to the offence committed.'

'I would never go beyond that,' Katz assured him.

'I accept that as the truth,' Foy said solemnly, reaching out with his right hand. 'Can we shake hands?'

Katz replied with a negative shake of his head. 'Possibly in three months' time if the truce between us holds.'

Dissatisfied with this, Foy nodded and walked out of the jailhouse.

Sitting with Katz and Hyer in the hotel, Aretha, having been told of Foy's peace offering, frowned as she asked, 'What do you make of it, Jorje?'

Waiting until Miguel placed their meals in front of them,

giving Katz a deferential little bow as he did so, Katz then responded to Aretha's question. 'It is not easy to answer that. Foy has recently lost a few men while not advancing his plans in any way. Probably he has decided there is little sense in continuing along the same trail.'

'You think he may revise his plans, Jorje?'

'I see that as the likeliest outcome,' Hyer spoke up.

'I agree,' Katz said in support of his deputy. 'Foy is not a young man, which has me go some way towards seeing his proposal as genuine. He may not be content to just make the most of what he now has. No doubt his ambition remains unaffected, but the cost of continuing it is a deterrent. However, there is something we must not overlook. Something that is not directly connected with Clement Foy.'

'Bartholomew Cusick,' Aretha breathed the name out as a sigh.

'Good thinking, Aretha,' Katz complimented her. 'Cusick has been lying low, but I don't doubt that a cunning guy like him will have been planning a way back. If Foy does take a back seat, which is likely, then Cusick will rise again.'

'And you will be caught in the middle,' Aretha predicted.

'That about sums it up, Aretha.'

'Tell me about this Bartholomew Cusick *hombre*,' Hyer earnestly requested.

Things took a nasty turn when Clement Foy returned to the Six Bar Six ranch house. Initially, Abraham, Foy's son, was pleased to learn that his father had returned from town with Ray Wilding.

'We can hold our heads high again now,' Abraham thankfully said.

Then Agnes Foy asked her husband a question. 'Did this Katz man cause you any problems, Clement?'

'He did not, and he will not do so at any time in the future, Agnes.'

Clapping his hands together in delight, Abraham praised his father. 'You fixed him real good, sir. Well done. You let him know who is boss around here.'

'That is far from what occurred, Abraham. Sheriff Katz and I had a most civilized discussion. He has given me his word that the only action he takes against anyone from the Six Bar Six will be strictly according to law.'

The boy, whose arguments were always potent but put forward studiously rather than emotionally, became increasingly angry as he posed a question. 'I am of a mind that it would be extremely foolish to trust a drifter such as Katz.'

'It is quite wrong of you to question your father, Abraham,' Agnes reprimanded her son.

'It is important that we learn every detail of what took place between him and Katz in town, Mother,' Abraham insisted before addressing his father once again. 'And what concessions did you make in return for the favours you secured from a vagrant gunslinger, sir?'

'A very important concurrence that is the only option in the current situation, son. From this day forth our business activities will be confined to modest improvements to the ranch as it now is.'

'But you are the big man in this district, sir. What about the schemes we have discussed that will enlarge the Six Bar Six enormously, boost our wealth beyond all measure, and give you invincible power?'

'It is prudent to let our empire building fall by the wayside, Abraham.'

'Turn the other cheek!' Abraham scoffed. 'You have always referred to that passage in the Bible as showing weakness that will encourage others to take advantage.'

'Abraham, what has happened to you?' the boy's mother queried in a quivering voice. 'This is not like you. You have always been a dutiful, respectful son, and you should apologize to your father.'

'That is something that I cannot do in the prevailing circumstances, Mother.'

Distressed rather than angered by his son's attitude, Clement Foy elucidated. 'Confronting Sheriff Jorje Katz is a very different proposition to taking on Sheriff Ike Rownton, Abraham.'

'You may be afraid of him, sir, but Sil Sontanna will not be.'

'I will not tolerate having my son call me a coward, Abraham,' Foy warned in a controlled tone. 'It is inappropriate to bring Sontanna into this discussion. He is working for me and will obey any instructions that I give him.'

'So we give up, back away from one stranger in our town?' Abraham shouted, his face purpling with rage.

'Abraham!' his father roared, his patience exhausted. 'I will not permit you to—'

He broke off in exasperation as his son hurriedly left the room, stamping his feet in fury as he went.

'What have I done, Mother?' Foy questioned his wife. 'I love that boy.'

'We both love our child, Clem,' she consoled him.

'But I have let him down. Now we have lost him.'

'That isn't true,' she insisted. 'He has gone off to bed now and will have calmed down by morning.

'I shall pray to the Lord that he will.'

'This is a surprise visit,' Cusick said as he answered the knock on his front door, asking humorously, 'Are you selling seed door to door now, Zac?'

'It is a serious matter that brings me here, Bart,' Zac Horton emphasized. 'Might I come in?'

Moving to one side, Cusick made a sweeping movement with his arm for Horton to enter, saying, 'Come in by all means, *Councillor* Horton.'

'I haven't come here to be the victim of sarcasm, Cusick. Are you prepared to have a sensible debate?'

'That depends,' Cusick replied dubiously. 'If I remember correctly, the last time we spoke was when you joined the other side. Why should I converse with a traitor, Horton?'

'Because that is over and done with. It is finished, Bart.'

'The new council has been dissolved?' Cusick asked with a squeal of shocked glee.

'No, no but I will be resigning soon. Harland is leading us in the wrong direction. I don't like what is taking place as it will mean us traders in the town will be footing the bill for his grandiose plans.'

'But why come to me? I am just one man against the whole world right now.'

'Nevertheless, you are the only man who can save this town, Bart, and things are changing fast,' Horton excitedly explained. 'What I have come here to tell you is that Clement Foy has given up. He is no longer a threat, Bart.'

Astonished by this, Cusick inquired, 'It is difficult to believe that Foy with all his might is ready to drop his campaign to have full control of this town, of the territory! How could this happen?'

'Jorje Katz is responsible. He has put the fear of Moses into Foy. Katz is the strong man in Singing River now. I am prepared to stay with the new council while feeding you information, Bart.'

'That would be really useful,' a thoughtful Cusick agreed. 'I have put together a scheme to regain power here, and as you want to help me I will see that you are well rewarded. You have relit my fire, Zac.'

Horton considered it practical to issue a warning. 'Remember the time will come when you will have to deal with Katz.'

'Leave that man to me,' Cusick replied confidently.

Any day now Johnny Lyng would come riding into town. That would alter everything in his favour. Lyng would have no problem in taking care of Katz and then Cusick was prepared to pay to have him to stay in Singing River while he put everything else to rights. Not that he was going to risk telling Horton about this.

He would rejoice to see the effect it would have on Aretha Ryland when Katz was gunned down. He had a score to settle with her because of her attitude towards him of late. With another manager already picked for the Stageline Hotel, he would then throw Aretha out on to the street.

'I'll be off then,' Horton said, breaking in on Cusick's thoughts.

'Goodnight, Zac. Thank you for coming to me with your offer to help.'

'Which you accept?' Horton paused to apprehensively inquire.

'Most gladly,' Cusick enthused.

Despite the late hour the Goldliner Saloon was noisy with music, laughter and the raised voices of drunks. Remaining until late in case trouble should occur, Katz had let Hyer go off duty. His deputy, who had taken on the job with a keen sense of loyalty, had protested before eventually leaving. Carmencita, still happy from the time they had spent together earlier, had managed to spend several snatched moments with him. Moments that neither of them had wanted to end.

Gradually the tempo of revelry started to slow. As the raucous clientele streamed past him on the way out, Katz stood by the swing doors ready to deal with any ruckus whether it happened inside or outside of the saloon. When the place had emptied Carmencita walked over to stand beside him.

'Phew! What a night!' she exclaimed. 'Are you leaving now, Jorje?'

He nodded. 'I'll take a look around outside, then I'll be on my way.'

'I would like to say thanks once more for the wonderful time I had today.'

About to tell her that no thanks were needed as he had also enjoyed the day, he was taken aback as she took a step forwards and kissed him. Quickly turning, she walked swiftly away. Standing for a minute or two watching her go, a slightly dazed Katz went slowly out through the batwing doors. He became his usual alert self as two figures walked out of the darkness.

'It's Sheriff Katz. Good evening, Sheriff.'

It was Meredith Harland and Preacher Donne who joined him under the light of the naphtha lamp outside the saloon. He greeted them jokingly with. 'Good evening? Good night would serve better. This is a late hour for two respectable gentlemen to be prowling about town.'

'Council business, Sheriff, council business,' Isaac Donne informed him with a smile. 'Will you join us on our walk homewards?'

'To do so would give me pleasure,' Katz responded. 'But I must stay a while to make certain all is quiet and peaceful.'

'We understand and appreciate your diligence, Jorje,' Harland said as he gave his shoulder a friendly pat.

'Goodnight to you.'

Katz bid them both goodnight and they left him. The night around him was undisturbed apart from the occasional scampering of a night creature. Satisfied, he was about to move on when a harsh voice called his name from the darkness.

'Katz!'

Aware of the threat in the call and that he was a target in the light of the lamp, Katz drew his six-shooter and dropped flat on the boardwalk. A shot was fired from the darkness. He fired at the flash made by the gun as a bullet thudded into the wooden fascia of the saloon above his head. Rising up into a crouch he moved out of the light into the shadows and waited.

Nothing stirred but then the batwing doors were pushed outwards and Carmencita stepped out.

'Are you there? Are you all right, Jorje?'

'Go back inside, Carmencita,' he called, standing up.

Not doing as she was told, Carmencita alarmed him by running to his side. But there were no more shots from the darkness. Giving her a brief one-armed hug, he whispered. 'Stay here.'

Making his way cautiously towards where he had seen the flare of the gun, he realized that Carmencita was following him. Conscious that it would endanger her and him if he stopped to send her back, he walked on, stopping as he almost tripped over a body lying on the ground. A breathless Harland and Donne came running up.

'I got him,' Katz announced in the poor light, indicating the body.

'Who is it?' Harland asked before dropping to one knee and striking a match.

As the match flared to reveal that the body was that of a

well-dressed young man, Preacher Donne drew a wheezing intake of breath. 'Dear Father in Heaven, it is Abraham Foy.'

'What is he to Clement Foy?' Katz asked.

'He is Foy's only child.' Getting to his feet, Harland answered Katz's question. 'There's going to be hell to pay now, Jorje.'

'Abraham tried to gun the sheriff down from the dark, Meredith. You and me can bear witness to that,' Donne applied logic to a situation that defied reason.

'That will make no difference when Foy learns what has happened,' Harland predicted.

'Why would a boy like him do such a thing?' Carmencita, who had turned away from the body when Harland's match had flared, asked.

'That is a really mystery,' Donne pondered. 'The boy is an intellectual who I doubt had ever touched a gun nor wanted to.'

'He sure touched one tonight, Isaac,' Harland pointed out.

'But why, Meredith?'

'We won't find out standing out here in the night,' Harland stated the obvious. He told Carmencita. 'You go inside, miss, there is nothing you can do out here. I will fetch "Barber" Shilton up here to deal with the body.'

'He won't be pleased being called out at this time of night,' Donne remarked.

'Dangle ten cents in front of "Barber" and he'd turn out at any time of the day and night in a blizzard,' Harland opined.

'I will ride out to the Six Bar Six to tell Foy what has happened,' Katz decided.

'NO!' Harland shouted the word. 'That would be the wrong move to start with. This situation has to be handled with great care. Are you up to riding out to inform Foy right now, Isaac?'

'I can do it, Meredith.'

'Good. Then you be on your way, Sheriff. We'll all meet in the morning to discuss the best way forward. Take the young lady away from here.'

Putting an arm around Carmencita's shoulders, Katz walked her to the doors of the saloon, where he bade her goodnight.

Before he could leave her she grabbed one of his arms with both hands, pleading, 'Foy will be out for vengeance over this, and he is a terrible man when he is angry. You will have to be extra careful, Jorje.'

'I am always careful,' he assured her.

'Promise me that you will.'

'I promise.'

Easing her in through the doors he hurried away. He slowed his pace as he saw the shadowy figures of Harland and Donne walking ahead. After the recent event he preferred to be alone. He was walking down the opposite side of the street to the Stageline Hotel when he heard Aretha call his name.

He stopped, waiting as she ran across the road to him. Her normally elegantly styled hair was slightly awry and she was clad in a long chemise. This had Katz guess that she had been woken from her sleep, most probably by the gunfire. Her first words proved him correct.

'Thank the Good Lord that you are safe, Jorje. I heard shooting and was dreadfully worried.'

'Go back to bed, Aretha, everything is fine.'

'Was anyone hurt?' she inquired in a shaky voice, careful to use the word 'hurt' rather than 'killed'.

To avoid answering her question he said. 'I will call on you first thing in the morning and tell you what happened.'

'Can't you tell me now?'

'It is late, so it is best to leave it until the morning,' he said.

Disappointed, she was walking slowly away but then stopped and turned to ask. 'Was that saloon girl involved in what happened just now?'

'Carmencita? Yes, she was there but not involved in any way.'

'Are you certain of that?' Aretha asked. 'I want you to take care. Do you trust her?'

'Completely.'

She was moving away once more and he called to her, 'Goodnight, Aretha.'

'Goodnight.'

Katz was only just able to catch her low-pitched, disheartened response.

Arriving at the Six Bar Six ranch house had been a traumatic experience for Isaac Donne. There was no way that he could phrase the tragic news in a way that wouldn't devastate Abraham Foy's parents. He had to rouse them from their beds by thumping on the door, and they came to open the door sleepily and hastily dressed. But the whole episode became farcical and took on even more anguish when Agnes Foy smiled when he had finished telling them that their son was dead.

'It was good of you to come all the way out here, Preacher Donne,' she calmly advised him. 'However, there has been a mistake. Abraham has been in his bed for the last two hours or more. I will fetch him down.'

When his wife had left the room, Clement Foy looked at the preacher stony-faced and unspeaking. This built up the tension in the room to badly affect the already bothered Donne, who welcomed hearing footsteps coming down the stairs. But his relief was short-lived.

'He is not there. His bed hasn't been slept in,' an ashen-faced Agnes Foy came into the room to report in a strangled voice.

Able to save her from falling as her legs gave way, Donne lowered her gently into an armchair. Her husband dashed across the room to return with a glass of whiskey, supporting her with an arm around her neck while holding the glass to her lips. Then he looked beseechingly up at Donne.

Aware that he was about to witness a sight that he dreaded most of all – that of a man of strong character breaking down – he forced himself to look in Foy's direction.

With tears streaming down his sagging cheeks, the rancher sobbed as he asked, 'When Agnes is feeling a little stronger, will you kneel in prayer with us, Preacher Donne?'

'Of course I will,' Donne replied softly, placing what he vainly hoped was a comforting hand on Foy's shoulder.

TEN

The funeral of Abraham Foy was a strictly private affair viewed from a far distance by interested townsfolk. There was no gathering after the burial, with only Sil Sontanna returning with Clement and Agnes Foy to the ranch house. It was an uncomfortable little group.

'You should lie down and rest, Agnes,' Foy advised his wife.

When the bereaved mother had left the room, Foy turned to Sontanna. 'There will be no rest for me until the death of my son has been avenged.'

Raising both eyebrows, Sontanna asked. 'Katz?'

'Katz,' Foy confirmed.

'What of the pact you made with him, Clem?'

'At no time did I agree to the murder of my son, so that agreement no longer stands.'

Sontanna chose his words carefully. 'We have no details of how Abraham died. I understand Katz has arranged for an inquiry to be held by Judge Handley.'

Foy dismissed this with a snort of disgust. 'Handley was Cusick's man. His verdicts can be bought cheaply. Harland and Donne will support Jorje Katz.'

'I take it that you are asking me to go up against Katz, Clem?'

'That is exactly what I am asking. Do you have some objection?'

'No,' Sontanna conveyed his doubt with a nuance on his one-word answer. 'What occurs to me is that you will be in big trouble if Katz proves to be faster than me. I always fight fair.'

'On this occasion you are to make sure that you win, regardless of what it takes.'

Having been more apprehensive than ever since Katz had related to her the circumstances in which he had shot Abraham Foy, Aretha Ryland's anxiety increased fourfold when she saw Sil Sontanna rein up on the opposite side of the street to the hotel. Not dismounting, he beckoned to a boy who ran over to him. Sontanna said something to the boy and reached into his pocket for a coin and passed it to him.

The boy ran off down the street while Sontanna dismounted, hitched his horse to a rail then leaned against a building and rolled a cigarette. Desperate to learn where this little scene was likely to lead, Aretha stepped out of the hotel and watched the boy reach the jailhouse and go inside.

Both Katz and Hyer became instantly alert as the jailhouse door was suddenly opened, then relaxed when a boy walked in and up to where Katz sat behind his desk.

'What can we do for you, kid?' Katz inquired.

'A man asked me to tell you that he's waiting for you up the street, Sheriff.'

Katz and Hyer exchanged glances. Katz asked. 'Does this man have a name?'

'He said his name is Som . . . Sombr . . . Son—'

Katz interrupted to end the boy's dilemma. 'Is his name Sontanna?'

'That's it.'

'Well done. You run along and tell him I'll be there.'

'It looks like we have a problem, Jorje,' Hyer drawled.

'I have a problem, not you, Fernando, you stay in here until I come back,' Katz stated. 'Sontanna is a proud man who will be alone.'

'It could well be a mistake to rely on that supposition,' Hyer warned. 'Play it safe by letting me make my way along behind the buildings.'

'Your offer is very much appreciated but I want to do this my way, Fernando,' Katz said as he stood to take his six-gun from its holster and spin the chamber.

'Then I will not interfere in any way, and I wish you well, Jorje,' Hyer said, walking to the door with Katz and shaking him by the hand before he left.

News of a pending challenge between gunfighters travels fast, Katz acknowledged to himself as he started a slow walk through the town's deserted main street. With each step he took and there was still no sign of Sontanna, Katz's dread increased that the confrontation would take place where Aretha would witness it.

His worst fears were realized outside of Meredith Harland's office when Sontanna stepped out into the street and stood waiting opposite the hotel.

Steps not faltering, Katz continued until coming to a halt a short distance from Sontanna, who said. 'You know why I am here, Katz.'

'I can probably guess.'

'As top hand at the Six Bar Six I am here to avenge Abraham Foy, the boy you murdered.'

'That isn't what you believe, Sontanna. You are the hired help doing what his master has told him to do.'

'That isn't so, Katz.'

'Then you had better make your move,' Katz said letting

his whole body relax in the manner which prepared him for an ultra-fast draw.

At that moment he caught from the corner of his eye a movement in the narrow gap between two buildings to his right. Instantly alert to a second source of immediate danger, he stayed focused on Sontanna while remaining aware of what might be happening to his right.

Katz was then distracted by Carmencita coming out of the passageway to shout, 'There's a rifle on the roof to your left, Jorje!'

Taking advantage of Katz's diversion, Sontanna went for his gun. Katz beat him to the draw, and there was the sound of two weapons firing almost simultaneously; the rifle up high to Katz's right and Katz's own gun. Sontanna slowly collapsed without having triggered a shot.

Relying on the sound of the rifle for direction, Katz swung to his right and fired high. His instinctive side had clicked in as always in a crisis, and a rifle came spiralling down from a flat roof, followed by the body of a man that sent up a cloud of dust as it thudded on to the street.

Reholstering his gun, Katz turned, intending to thank Carmencita for her timely intervention; his whole body went icily cold as he saw her lying face down in a pool of blood. He dropped on both knees beside her as Aretha came running up.

Hands to her mouth in horror at the sight, Aretha croaked, 'Is she dead, Jorje?'

'No, but she is badly hurt,' he replied.

'Let's carry her over to the hotel,' Aretha stammered, still in shock.

Lifting Carmencita up in his arms, he said. 'You fetch the doc. Please hurry.'

Many people were out in the street by then but Katz was

barely aware of them as he carried Carmencita across to the hotel. Going in, he kicked the door of a side room open and went in to lay the injured girl on the bed.

Minutes later the old doctor came into the room with Aretha. Wasting no time he sliced open Carmencita's shirt to the waist to reveal that her abdomen had been torn open by a rifle bullet. Hands covered in blood he expertly examined the wound, while Katz and Aretha anxiously looked on, the latter quietly crying.

'The poor girl,' she whispered to Katz. 'I am ashamed of the things that I thought and said about her.'

'She needs your prayers now,' Katz softly told her.

'Save your prayers for later,' the doc sadly advised, raising his head. 'The dear child has just slipped away.'

Katz took a step closer to the bed, bowing his head in silence as he looked down at Carmencita, while Aretha slumped on a chair, weeping.

At the well-attended funeral of Carmencita Fernandez, an already grieving Katz had been further moved when a young Mexican girl from the Goldliner Saloon delivered a eulogy at the graveside that was a summing up of Carmencita's courage and kindness. In tears at the end, the girl said, 'Although the kind of life we lead is not our choice, girls like us are frowned upon. Even so, no one can say a bad word about my dear friend Carmencita.'

Katz found it easy to mutely agree with every word. He recalled how Carmencita had told him of her yearning for a better life. All she had found was an early death. Had she died in different circumstances they would have overwhelmed him, but knowing she had sacrificed herself for him was destroying.

It made it difficult to show or to take any interest when

attending the council meeting that Meredith Harland had called the day following her burial. The townsfolk had been invited, and Katz was very conscious of Aretha's presence.

'What action will we now take against Clement Foy?' Jeremiah Sutton asked.

'I would remind this meeting that Clement Foy has just lost his only child,' Isaac Donne said, standing to sweep a stern look over everyone assembled there.

'Foy caused the death of a young girl,' Ebenezer Forest protested. 'Are we to consider the death of Foy's son as more lamentable than the death of a saloon girl?'

'I am deeply offended by that question,' a visibly upset Isaac Donne said.

'No one here can doubt Preacher Donne's divinity,' Harland intervened. 'Councillor Sutton has raised the question of what should be done in relation to the recent outrages in the town. That is an important question. Conversely, there is a more pressing matter which has prompted me to call this meeting.'

'What could be more urgent than dealing with Clement Foy?' Zac Horton angrily inquired.

Remaining calm, though obviously having difficulty doing so, Harland replied. 'The answer to that is that I have learned Bartholomew Cusick has placed a motion before Judge Handley that declares this council unlawful and requires it to be dissolved. It also states that the sheriff we appointed has no legal standing and must be placed on trial for the murders of Abraham Foy, Sil Sontanna, David Rossi, and Carmencita Fernandez.'

Hearing this brought a breathless silence to the community. Sitting beside Katz, Hyer whispered, 'I suppose Rossi is the guy with the rifle on the roof.'

Katz nodded numbly as Sutton got to his feet to ask, 'What

do you say we should do, Meredith?'

'My opinion is that we should carry on as we are. I will, of course, take a vote on that, but it would be impossible to continue without the support of Sheriff Katz. Would we have your support, Jorje?'

Every head turned to Katz as he got to his feet to answer. 'I will not leave Singing River until law and order prevails.'

'Then I second Meredith,' Jeremiah Sutton shouted.

The motion to continue the new council was put to the vote and passed unanimously.

'I am sorry to intrude on you at this most grievous time,' Cusick said timorously as he stood at the ranch house door.

'Then why are you here?' Clement Foy asked brusquely.

'I came because I feel it important to both of us to discuss the present situation,' Cusisk answered earnestly.

So earnestly that Foy stood back from the door saying, 'Then you had best come in.'

Inside he surprised Cusick by asking him to be seated then pouring them both a glass of whiskey. Then he suggested, 'You went to the trouble of riding out here, Cusick, so it is right that you speak first.'

'Thank you. I want you to know that I have placed a motion before Judge Handley to have Harland's council declared unlawful. I am sure the result will be that it is dissolved and I shall be re-installed as the democratically elected mayor.'

'I congratulate you. That is a good move,' Foy said, warming to the subject. 'The only obstacle I envisage is Katz. As I learned to my cost, he is difficult to remove. But I do have a plan to deal with him.'

'What is that?' Cusick forced himself to ask, wanting to put his own idea forward.

'Once the council is dissolved, you as mayor can remove him from his role as sheriff. Then I will send for a US marshal. While we wait for him to arrive we simply prepare a dossier pinning the recent deaths on Katz.'

'I like that scheme,' Cusick lied, 'but I fear that it will take too long. May I tell you of an arrangement that I have already made?'

'Go ahead, Bart.'

'Have you heard of Johnny Lyng?'

'I wouldn't think there is anyone out West who hasn't.'

'Well, he's on his way here, should arrive at any time. Katz will be no match for him.'

Pursing his lips dubiously, Foy said. 'It will have to be done legitimately, so to speak. To make a new start we need to be seen as law-abiding and responsible people.'

'I have used Lyng before and he knows how to fix it so that Katz will be in the wrong.'

'That's great! Let me refill your glass, we'll talk some more and then shake hands on a relationship for mutual benefit,' Foy said with a pleased smile.

'At the meeting this afternoon you said that you wouldn't leave Singing River until order had been restored,' Aretha falteringly reminded Katz. 'Does that mean you have no intention of settling here?'

It was early evening and they sat together on a low hill, an idyllic spot just outside the town. At Aretha's suggestion they had strolled there to share a much-needed break from the hostility and violence that had plagued, and still threatened, Singing River. Aware that he had been downcast since the death of Carmencita, she hoped to help him come to terms with that tragic event.

'Not having settled anywhere at any time in my life,' Katz

responded gravely, 'not long ago it had occurred to me that Singing River was the ideal place for a man to put down roots.'

'But no more?'

'Things have changed, Aretha.'

'Carmencita?'

Unusually for Katz, his emotions were discernible when he answered this question. 'Carmencita was a remarkable person. In the short time I knew her we became close friends. Our relationship had never once strayed into what is generally regarded as the man and woman kind. Regardless of that, the circumstances of her death mean that she will forever haunt me.'

'Making it impossible for you to remain here.'

'Not necessarily so, but it will play a part in any decision that I may make.'

Planning to have him expand on this theme, Aretha realized that he was staring down to where the trail into Singing River ran along at the foot of the hill. Following his gaze, she saw a lone rider making his way slowly into town.

'Do you know that man, Jorje?' she inquired.

He nodded. 'That is Johnny Lyng, a ruthless killer.'

'Heading for town.' She sighed. 'I was hoping that our troubles were over.'

'From what I know of Lyng they haven't yet begun, Aretha,' Katz grimly predicted.

Though annoyed by Johnny Lyng lying back in a chair with his booted feet resting on an expensive oak table, Cusick managed to remain affable as he poured two drinks and passed one to his guest.

Raising his glass to all but drain it with one gulp, Lyng asked, 'Who is the target, Cusick?'

'The local sheriff.'

Dragging his feet off the table, Lyng sat upright with a jolt. 'The message you sent didn't mention a sheriff. I don't normally mess with the law, Cusick, but if I have to my services come dear.'

'He isn't officially a sheriff but someone appointed by a non-elected council.'

'That's different. Is he a local man?'

'No. He arrived here a short time ago. You may know him; he's a gunfighter by the name of Jorje Katz.'

Relaxing and about to place his feet back on the table, Lyng let his booted feet hit the floor with a bang. 'I know of him. You have got yourself a hard man there, Cusick.'

'Can you take him?'

'I can take him.'

'Good,' Cusick acknowledged before adding, 'My position here in Singing River necessitates it being done in a way that does not reflect on me.'

'You worry too much, Cusick. I will create a mock vendetta with Katz that will have the people of your town recognize that he deserved to be shot.'

'That will do nicely,' Cusick chuckled.

Late in the evening on which he had seen Johnny Lyng ride into Singing River, Katz entered the Goldliner Saloon with Hyer on their regular nightly patrol. Katz was relieved to find the place fairly quiet. Since the death of Carmencita he couldn't bear to linger in the saloon. His intention of taking a quick look around and then leaving was frustrated when a raised voice addressed him.

'Well, well, if it isn't Jorje Katz, and wearing a silver star! What sort of a town is this to make a *bandido* like you sheriff?'

Katz turned to see a grinning Johnny Lyng leaning back in

an arrogant pose with his back against the bar, both elbows resting on it. His hands were just above the butts of the pair of Colt. 45s holstered on his twin, crossed gunbelts. A black Stetson tilted back from his forehead, he studied Katz through hooded eyes.

'Singing River has no need of bounty hunters, Lyng,' Katz said. 'You are not welcome here.'

This exchange had attracted the attention of all those present. Games were put on hold and conversations abandoned by people avid for the situation to develop.

'I guess you're the only one not to welcome me, Katz, and the reason why is what I have in here,' Lyng patted his shirt pocket as he taunted Katz. 'You are wanted in New Mexico for killing a whole family, man, woman and two little children.' He paused for effect as many of those listening gasped in horror. Then he patted his shirt pocket once more. 'In there is a handbill offering a handsome sum for you, dead or alive. I aim to collect that award.'

'Your time is up in this town, Lyng,' an unimpressed Katz said. 'You ride out tonight, or I will come looking for you.'

This made Lyng laugh loudly. 'That will save me the trouble of looking for you, Katz. I am staying here overnight as a guest of Mayor Bartholomew Cusick. You will have to come out in the street at some time tomorrow. When you do, I'll be waiting.'

Katz turned and walked out of the saloon, followed by Hyer who was obviously puzzled by the sheriff's sudden departure.

It was after midnight in the Stageline Saloon. All of the guests and staff had retired for the night. Katz, Hyer and Doc Walpole sat in with Aretha in her private room, each of them holding a glass of brandy toddy as they earnestly discussed the latest crisis. Katz's three companions had accepted without question that Lyng had been lying when claiming that he was wanted for murder.

'I take it that this Lyng is fast, Jorje?' the old doc queried.

'He's fast, real fast, Doc.'

'Not fast enough to worry you,' Hyer expressed his faith in Katz.

'Lyng doesn't worry me,' Katz said. 'My regret is that I came here to put an end to my old way of life, but I can't break away from it. I just didn't anticipate another situation like this. Lyng is Cusick's hole card. He intends to use him to re-establish himself as mayor and take over Singing River. Anyway, I'm going to get some sleep. Come on, Fernando.'

Aretha followed Katz and Hyer to the door, and the latter walked a few yards away so that she and Katz could talk. She asked, 'Will you be leaving Singing River tomorrow, Jorje?'

'I'll answer that question after I have met Lyng tomorrow,' Katz told her. 'Goodnight, Aretha.'

At 10 o'clock the next morning Katz, having reached a decision, left the jailhouse. Hyer kept the door open to repeat the offer of help he had been making for the past two hours.

'I'll just be in a position to act if Lyng tries any tricks, Jorje.'

'He won't,' Katz said as he walked, staying alert for a sighting of Lyng on the deserted street.

There had been no sign of Lyng by the time he reached Al Pertain's place and went in. Saddling his stallion, he led it out into the still empty street and swung up into the saddle to ride back down to the jailhouse. He hitched the horse outside and was stepping up on to the boardwalk when he sensed the presence of another person on the street.

It was Johnny Lyng walking slowly and casually towards

him. They both stopped as if by mutual consent, with Lyng giving Katz a smile that was almost friendly.

Losing the smile, he spoke seriously. 'This is a special occasion, Jorje. We are the remaining two top gunslingers about to fight a duel to the death. Right this moment we are making history. Tomorrow we will most probably be on the front pages of many newspapers.'

'It's a pity you won't be around to read them, Johnny.'

Lyng smiled again, a genuine smile. 'We have both outlived our era, so that thought means nothing to me. With the past we knew gone forever there is no future for either of us.'

Recognizing the truth of this, Katz was dejected. But his gunfighter's instinct was working well and he concentrated as he heard Lyng speaking in a different way.

'Right now, Jorje, I would like to shake your hand and walk away, but that awesome thing called pride prevents me from doing so. What I would like to say—'

As Lyng broke off speaking he went for both his guns. Aware that this was about to happen. Katz drew and fired, feeling a bullet from Lyng crease his ribs. Giving the last smile he would ever smile, Lyng collapsed slowly but in a manner that said he was dead before he hit the dirt.

Katz walked to his horse. He had one foot in the stirrup when Harland and his councillors emerged to crowd around him, Meredith Harland begged him not to leave. When Katz insisted that he was going, they all shook hands with him before he mounted up. Then Hyer came out to bid him farewell.

Riding slowly up the street, ignoring the body of Lyng as he passed it, with the pain in his side increasing fast, he reined up as Aretha came out of the hotel and ran to him. Looking at his blood-soaked shirt she pleaded with him, 'You are badly hurt, get down and come in. I will fetch Doc Barlow.'

'I'm sorry. I am leaving.'

'Will I never see you again, Jorje?'

'Never is a long time. Goodbye, Aretha,' Katz said, moving his horse away; riding on up the street he left the town without once looking back.

Half an hour later, still riding at a slow pace with no destination in mind, Katz was irresistibly drawn to the hill that he had visited with Carmencita. Reaching the brow he could sense her presence and a feeling of peace settled on him. As he continued to sit in the saddle looking out at a hazy distant horizon his mind, which had been disturbed since he had arrived in Singing River, suddenly cleared.

Though ready to move on he sat unmindful of passing time as he captured the full experience of what Carmencita had felt when they were here together. This was such a profound emotion that Katz could now fully understand how it had meant so much to her. It occurred to him, easing his grief as it did so, that she had now found what she had so desperately sought after. Something that she would never have been able to find in the kind of life that circumstances had forced on her on earth.

Feeling better about everything, folding his bandanna and putting it inside of his shirt to staunch the bleeding, he rode down the hill and went on his way.

'Miss Ryland, there are some gentlemen here to see you,' Miguel announced after knocking on the door of her private room.

'Thank you, Miguel. Please say that I will be with them in a few minutes,' Aretha said, wondering who her visitors could be.

Soon after Lyng's body had been taken away, Aretha, needing to be alone to shed tears that had been building up since Katz had left her, had gone to her room. Getting to her feet she went to a mirror to discover that there was no way she could conceal the reddening of her eyes from weeping. Knowing that she would have to brave facing whoever it was waiting to see her, she opened the door of her room and walked out to find Meredith Harland and Isaac Donne waiting for her.

Both men were instantly aware of her signs of distress, something both tried to hide. Harland spoke first to inform her that, thanks to Katz, it seemed certain that life in Singing River would from now on be serene.

'Young Fernando Hyer is staying on if anyone should breach the law,' he announced before continuing with news that worried Aretha terribly. 'You will be pleased to hear that Bartholomew Cusick is leaving for good, and Clement Foy has been mellowed by the death of his son.'

Pleased to hear! Good God, that was the last thing she wanted to hear about Cusick. Straight after Katz had ridden away she was now about to lose both her employment and her home. This extra blow was shattering until she heard Harland carry on speaking.

'All of us councillors, with the exception of Zac Horton, have invested money to purchase this hotel from Cusick. Your position here is secure, Miss Ryland, if you wish to continue under the new owners.'

'I most certainly do, Mr Harland,' an immensely relieved Aretha responded. 'I am most grateful to you for retaining me.'

'We were praying that you would want to stay with us. I would like to say on my own behalf and that of my partners in this enterprise, that we consider ourselves fortunate indeed to have an efficient person such as yourself in charge.'

'Thank you, Mr Harland.'

'We look forward to a mutually profitable and amicable future together, Miss Ryland,' Harland said as he and Donne made their way to the door.

Opening the door, the two men were about to leave when Harland turned to step back inside, saying, 'I think you will want to see this, Miss Ryland.'

Intrigued, Aretha ran to stand beside Harland and Donne on the boardwalk. The street was busy as it would be on any day at that time, which had her puzzled as to what she had been called out for. Then her heart missed a beat before thumping wildly as she saw a lone rider approach, slumped sideways in the saddle. It was Jorje Katz.

She stood in the street and he reined up beside her. He looked exhausted and his shirt was a bloody mess. He managed a smile for her.

'I'll fetch the doc, Jorje,' she said. 'You were wise to come back to have that wound treated.'

'I need the doc,' he agreed, his voice hoarse. 'But that is not what brought me back.'

He didn't resist her help in getting him down from his horse, and stood unsteadily, using the stallion for support.

'What brought you back, Jorje?' she finally risked asking the question though still apprehensive as to what his answer would be.

'I realized that I had grown to like Singing River, Aretha.'

Anxious to go to fetch the doctor, she forced herself to ask. 'How long do you intend to stay?'

'Forever, if you will have me,' he replied.

Elated, she embraced him, mindless of his blood soaking into her expensive dress.